The Colleen Bawn
– the facts and the fiction.

William MacLysaght
The Tragic Story
of the
Colleen Bawn

ANVIL BOOKS

The Tragic Story of the Colleen Bawn
First published by Anvil Books in 1953
Reprinted 1964, 1970, 1971, 1975, 1978
This edition 1982
Copyright 1953 Anvil Books

The Collegians
adapted by Sigerson Clifford
First published by Anvil Books in 1964
Reprinted 1970, 1971, 1975, 1978
This edition 1982
© Copyright 1964 Anvil Books

ISBN 0 900068 60 4

Cover photograph: Bord Failte
Printed in Ireland by
The Leinster Leader Limited, Naas

❧ Contents

THE TRAGIC STORY OF THE COLLEEN BAWN

THE COLLEGIANS,
ADAPTED BY SIGERSON CLIFFORD

❧ Foreword

In the Autumn of 1819, the people of County Limerick were profoundly shocked by the barbarous murder of a young peasant girl.

The victim, Ellen Hanley, a mere child not quite sixteen years of age, was of outstanding beauty – in the Irish phrase, a *colleen bawn* (literally white girl but which might be more aptly translated as 'golden girl'). She was of a bright and friendly disposition which endeared her to all who knew her little world of Ballycahane and the nearby village of Croom in County Limerick.

On June 29, 1819, this young girl disappeared from the house of her uncle, John Connery, by whom she had been reared since the death of her mother when she was six years of age. From the time of her disappearance, nothing was heard of her until September 6, when her body was washed ashore at Moneypoint on the River Shannon, bearing unmistakable evidence that she had been murdered.

The appalling crime created feelings of horror and pity in everyone. Suspicion immediately pointed to Ellen Hanley's seducer who had gone through a form of marriage with her, and the coroner brought in a verdict of wilful murder against John Scanlan, son of one of the leading county families and recently a lieutenant in the Royal Marines, and Stephen Sullivan, his boatman and servant. Both fled immediately.

Two months later Scanlan was captured in the outhouse of his home, Ballycahane Castle. His trial, in March 1820, created a huge sensation, both on account of the high social position of his family and the extreme youth and beauty of his victim. He was defended by the famous Irish lawyer, Daniel O'Connell, the Liberator.

Two months after Scanlan's execution and ten months after the death of Ellen Hanley, Stephen Sullivan was still at large. He seemed to have vanished without trace. Actually he had gone to ground at Scartaglen in County Kerry, many miles away, and felt so safe in his new home that he actually married a local girl, the daughter of respectable parents, and 'settled down'.

Ironically, he came into collision with the law on a matter that had nothing to do with Ellen Hanley's death. He was charged with a crime of which he may indeed have been innocent and found himself in Tralee goal. But he was still safe. He had taken the precaution of assuming a new name and, so far, nobody dreamed of connecting a newly married man of steady habits with the murder on the Shannon. The account of how he was brought to trial was verified from official papers, given in the Appendix.

The first part of this book, *The Tragic Story of the Colleen Bawn* presents the authentic story of what happened. All the people mentioned are real people and the places can be found on any large-scale map. Author William MacLysaght was born at Cappamore, County Limerick, and has written many successful plays; his research covered every possible source of information.

Part two is Sigerson Clifford's adaptation of Gerald Griffin's popular story, *The Collegians*. As a young reporter of twenty-five Griffin covered the trials of Scanlan and Sullivan for the papers and in the novel they are thinly disguised under the names of Hardress Cregan and Danny Mann. Sullivan by the way, was not a hunchback as Danny is portrayed, but a well-built man. Ellen Hanley has her name changed to Eily O'Connor, but the other characters in the book, Lowry Looby, Fighting Poll of the Reeks, Myles na Gopaleen, Anne Chute, Dunat O'Leary and others are pure fiction. *The Collegians* brought Griffin immediate fame. Dion Boucicault staged it as a play, *The Colleen Bawn*, and Benedict used it for his opera, *The Lily of Killarney*.

Sigerson Clifford comes from Caherciveen, County Kerry. His plays have been staged in the Abbey Theatre and in Belfast and are highly popular with the amateur dramatic societies. Published work includes *Travelling Tinkers*, *Lascar Rock*, *Ballads of a Bogman*, *The Book of Irish Recitations* and *Legends of Kerry*.

❧ 1 *The Colleen Bawn*

She's come! She's come!
I wondered at first why a tenderer light
Added beauty today and new lustre tonight;
I wondered to see a fresh bloom on the flowers,
The laughter and joy that came with the hours:

IRISH BALLAD

THE TWO YOUNG MEN, who had just rounded a bend in the road, came to a full stop under an overhanging wayside tree. Both of the men were of good height and physique. One of them was obviously in his very early twenties, well dressed, and carried a fowling piece in the crook of his arm; the other, a little older, was more roughly attired, but carried himself with a certain air of easy independence.

'Is that the cottage, Sullivan?' said the younger man, pointing to a house some distance down the road.

'That's the place, Master John,' replied the other. 'What are you going to do now?'

'I'm damned if I know," was the reply. 'We have no excuse for calling there—at least that I can think of.'

'Huh!' said the man referred to as Sullivan, in a derisive tone, which showed that he was on terms of easy familiarity with his companion. 'What's to prevent us from making an excuse?'

'Well, what's the notion in your head—as you're so inventive?'

'Why not call in to Connery to take your measure for a pair of riding boots?' said Sullivan. 'You know we can hardly say we've lost our way, as he knows us so well,' he added with a grin.

'Not a bad shot,' replied the other; 'but I have a new pair of riding boots; and, if I hadn't, I doubt that he could make them—Steady!' he added, abruptly. 'Luck is on our side. There's a heavy shower coming on, and we can take refuge in the cottage.'

' "The devil's childre" again, Master John,' said Sullivan with a chuckle. As he spoke, he was amazed to see his companion lift his fowling piece and discharge it over their heads, at nothing in particular. 'What are you up to?' he continued. 'Trying to shoot down the rain?'

'No need to do that—it's coming down anyway,' was the reply. 'That, Sullivan, is what's called "setting the stage"—or, if you like, preparing the ground. All is now ready for the entrance of the sportsman seeking shelter from the weather.'

'The devil a finer, Master John,' said Sullivan, ironically. 'I must think of that plan the next time I go coortin'.'

'Step it out, Sullivan,' said the other. 'There's the first of the rain, and it falls impartially on saints and sinners.'

'That leaves us no chance on either ticket,' said Sullivan.

As the two men approached the cottage door, the rain, which had been threatening, started to bucket down, and they had to run the last fifty yards. In response to their urgent knock, the door was opened by a man somewhat past middle age, who greeted them with a kindly 'Come in quick—ye'll be drowned!' Slamming the door against the driving rain, he turned to greet the newcomers, and exclaimed in surprise, 'Why, it's Lieutenant Scanlan and Stephen Sullivan. I'd no notion it was you were fowling, Master John, when I heard a shot some short time ago.'

Scanlan gave a significant smile in Sullivan's direction, as he answered : 'Well, Connery, we couldn't be caught by the rain in a better place—near friendly shelter.'

'Oh, you're welcome, indeed, Master John,' Connery replied. 'But you've got some of the rain. Push in to the fire—and you, Stephen, and dry yere clothes before the rain soaks in. Ellie!' he added, raising his voice, 'bring out two of the good chairs from the room there.'

In response to this request, there emerged from a room opening off the kitchen, a young girl with a chair in either hand. On her appearance, Scanlan hastily placed his gun against the wall and stepped forward, with a word of thanks and a smile, to relieve her of the chairs. He and Sullivan then seated themselves at the open fireplace, in which a brisk peat fire was burning.

The girl who had brought the chairs now stood near the window, fiddling with some things on the kitchen table, as if undecided whether to stay or retire. She was of medium height, very graceful build, and quite young—very little over the school-girl age. Her dress was simple, yet becoming; but all about her paled before the exquisite loveliness of her face, whose singular beauty was enhanced by a serene look of peculiar charm which contrasted delightfully with her evident youth. As Scanlan sat by the fire, his gaze constantly wandered to the girl, while Sullivan watched him furtively, with a half concealed ironic grin.

'Had you any luck with the fowling, Master John?' enquired Connery, who had now drawn over a chair for himself to the fire.

'Not a bit, Connery,' was the reply. 'I'm afraid the only birds the poachers have left around here are sparrows and jackdaws.'

'Aye. I'm afraid you're right,' said the other; 'and you know there's no sport in that game. The only rule the poachers work to is to plunder all they can for themselves, and the devil take anyone else.'

As the two men sat chatting about the prospects of sport in the locality, Scanlan's gaze continued to wander, and to any but a careless observer, it was evident that his mind was not on the conversation. Catching Sullivan's eye, he fixed him with a very meaning look, and exclaimed, suddenly : 'I say, Sullivan, what has become of our setter?'

'Good Lord, Master John,' said the other, with quick perception, 'I forgot him in the rush for shelter—and he's off his feed, not in such good shape. I hope I'll be able to find him wherever he's nosing about.'

'I'll give you a hand, Stephen,' said the good-natured Connery. 'Throw that old oil coat over your shoulders; this canvas bag will do me fine as the rain is clearing off.

As the two men left in search of the mythical dog, Scanlan gave a sigh of satisfaction at the success of his ruse, and turned towards the young girl at the other side of the room.

'Won't you come down to the fire, Miss Hanley?' he queried politely. 'You are making me feel like a disturber in the house.' As he spoke, he rose and held a chair ready for her—not very far from his own.

The girl accepted the proffered seat shyly, yet with a certain grace. 'You know my name,' she said. 'Nearly all the people around here call me "Connery," on account of living with Uncle John.'

'Oh, I know your name quite well,' said Scanlan, adding, boldly, 'and it has been a matter of regret with me for some time that I didn't know the lady who bore it.'

At this the girl coloured, looking somewhat confused, and seemed somewhat at a loss for a reply. Perceiving this, Scanlan continued : 'But we are neighbours, nearly. You know me, don't you?'

'Oh, yes,' she replied. 'I've known you for quite a time. I've seen you often in Croom, and I've seen you riding to the hunt a few times.'

'And what sort of a figure do I cut on horseback?' queried Scanlan. 'Did I leave a favourable impression on your mind?'

'You did, indeed,' answered the girl. 'I thought you looked fine, and I looked forward to seeing you again.' As this indiscreet confession slipped from her, Ellie Hanley realised that she had said too much, and added hastily : 'I love to see the huntsmen; they look so gay and dashing.'

'But were *all* the huntsmen the same to you?' said Scanlan, following up his advantage. 'Was there no *one* of them you would like best to see again?' As he spoke, he took the girl's shapely hand in his own, while he sought to hold her with his eyes.

Ellie Hanley paused, but made no attempt to withdraw her hand. 'Was there?' he repeated, softly, as he felt the girl's hand tremble slightly in his own. Then, at the sound of footsteps approaching the house, she raised her eyes, dropped them immediately, and murmured : 'There—there was !'

Just as the latch was lifted, Scanlan inclined his head quickly, whispered something hurriedly, and released her.

2 Gossip at the Inn

She is beautiful, and therefore to be woo'd
She is a woman, therefore to be won.
WILLIAM SHAKESPEARE

IT HAD BEEN A TIRING MORNING at the fair of Croom. The cattle on offer had sold slowly—mainly at poor prices, and when the two friends, having finished their business, met

12

outside the door of the village inn, they immediately adjourned to the cosy taproom.

The older of the two men, who had purchased the drinks, glanced sideways into his now empty tankard, and, with a sly glance at his friend, made a pretence of draining the empty vessel.

'Well, Meehaul,' he said, 'don't you think we'd better be shortening the road?'

'There's the devil's own hurry on you, Larry,' replied Meehaul. 'We're on foot now since before daybreak, and I think we're well entitled to take it easy for the rest of the day. What'll you have?' he added, rising to the bait.

'Well, I suppose a drop of the same again won't do us any harm,' said Larry. 'Y'know, I think the best pint in the village of Croom, or for that matter, in County Limerick, is kept here. She keeps good stuff, and, sign's on, it hasn't time to go stale or casky.'

'True for you,' agreed the other; and then, raising his voice to the shopwoman, who was serving a young girl at the grocery counter, he called, 'Hi! missis. Will you fill these again for us, like a good girl.'

'Just a minute, men,' replied the woman, 'until I give this young girl her messages, and I'll be with ye.'

'Powerful lot of cattle in the fair here to-day,' said Larry. 'Biggest fair I've seen in Croom this many a long day. How did your lot go?'

'Go—How the devil d'you think, but bad. A man had better be an ass to an apple-man than farming these days, and, mind you,' he added, 'things will be worse by all accounts. We're not out of the wood yet.'

'Faith, I'm sorry to say that I have to agree with you,' said Larry slowly. 'Eighteen-hundred-and-nineteen,' he mused, 'nearly four years since Waterloo, and the devil or Doctor Foster* never saw such bad times for the farmers.'

'Ah, it's the old story,' Meehaul agreed. 'While Boney was on the rampage the farmers were fine fellows. Now we can go to blazes.'

'Well, Meehaul,' said his friend, 'I don't think you'd expect a blast of the nightingale's song from a jackdaw, would you? And when you see gratitude from *any* Government, it's likely the cocks will be laying eggs. Tell me,' he

---

* A corruption of Doctor Faustus.

added with sudden interest, 'who's that young girl at the grocery counter?'

Oh, don't you know her?' said Meehaul, in some surprise.

'No. She's a fine looking youngster.'

'She's all that,' agreed Meehaul, casting an appreciative eye to where a young girl was gathering a number of small parcels from the counter into her basket. 'You know old Connery of Ballycahane?'

'The shoemaker?'

'The very man. Well, the youngster is his niece. Her name is Ellie Hanley.'

'Be damned,' said Larry, 'but she's a colleen bawn from head to toe. I wish a few of mine were like her—they wouldn't be long looking for husbands. Where did old Connery get her?'

'You remember Connery's sister, don't you, who married Hanley?'

'I do well, God rest her.'

'Well, this girl is her daughter; but she lives with the uncle.'

'How's that?'

'Well,' said Meehaul, a note of compassion creeping into his voice, 'after the poor mother died there some years ago, Hanley got married again, and Connery took Ellie to live with him.' He paused, shook his head, and added, 'The Hanleys are not well off, you know, and he finds it hard enough to drag along, poor devil, on his bit of stony land.'

'H-m. The daughter seems to be well looked after, anyhow.'

'Oh, she's all that. The apple of old Connery's eye—and the same may be said for all the lads around these parts.'

'Huh! I don't think too much admiration is very good for a young girl. It gives them empty notions, you know.'

'Well, no, then,' said Meehaul, 'that doesn't hold good in Ellie's case. She's a grand youngster, with no put-on, and a pleasant word for everybody. You know,' he added, 'she's not quite sixteen years of age yet, although she's such a fine whip of a girl.'

'H-m. Plenty of time to find a husband—which will be small trouble to her with those looks.'

'Listen to this,' said Meehaul, glancing around and lowering his voice to a confidential tone. 'Here's something that'll stagger you. Do you know who has a great eye after Ellie?'

'How the devil could I know?' said Larry impatiently, 'when I didn't even know her name until you told me now. *Who?*'

'John Scanlan!'

'Wh-what,' spluttered Larry, falling back a step, as if to get a better perspective on the news. *'Scanlan!* D'you mean young Scanlan of Ballycahane House?'

'Master John Scanlan of the Big House, if you please,' said Meehaul, ironically, 'lieutenant in the Royal Marines, and one of the leading young sportsmen in County Limerick.'

'Good-Lord-above!' said Larry, with great deliberation, as he gaped at his companion, who was evidently relishing the sensation which he had caused. 'God keep the child far away from that la-dee-daw—he means her no good.'

'Who are you telling it to?' replied Meehaul. He paused and then added with bitter contempt : *'The Scanlans and their crowd!* related to all the big pots in the country. His people wouldn't look at the side of the road poor Ellie Hanley walks on.'

Larry sighed. 'Ah, that's where the loss of her poor mother comes in. No one to advise the little girl.'

'No one, indeed,' agreed his friend. 'Old Connery wouldn't see a hole in a ladder—although he dotes on the little girl.'

'Tell me this,' queried Larry, 'why didn't they keep Scanlan in the Navy?'

'Oh, there I leave you,' said Meehaul. 'Now he's gallivanting around the country with the two qualifications the devil likes best in a young fellow—money in his pocket and nothing to do.'

'Well, we can only hope that God'll take care of His own.'

'Amen to that,' said Meehaul, fervently. 'Ellie Hanley is a good innocent girl, who sees no harm in anyone. If she had a grain of sense in her head, she'd put the width o' the ocean between herself and Scanlan.'

'Hi, missis!' he called suddenly, raising his voice. 'Are you forgetting all about your customers here?'

❧ 3 Flight

Oh, weep for the hour when to Eveleen's bower,
The Lord of the Valley with false vows came.
THOMAS MOORE

THE ROAD NEAR BALLYCAHANE was dark and deserted on
this night at the end of June, 1819, some two months after
the fair in the nearby village of Croom.

Not a sound disturbed the lonely countryside, save the
distant barking of a dog, which carried with uncanny
clearness from the farmhouse almost a mile distant, and
served but to emphasise the solemn stillness known only to
dwellers in the country.

Under the shelter of some over-hanging roadside trees
a young man was seated motionless on a horse, his presence revealed only by the sudden jingle of a bridle, as his
animal tossed its head impatiently. Suddenly, the sound of
footsteps was heard approaching.

'Is that you, Sullivan?' said the horseman, in a low but
impatient voice, as he peered towards the dim figure loom-
ing out of the darkness.

'Yes, Mr. Scanlan,' said the newcomer, in the same
guarded tone.

'What the devil kept you such a long time?'

'Well, I had to bide my time to deliver your note, until
I got old Connery out of the way—you told me to be
careful, didn't you?' he added, in challenging resentment.

'Yes—yes; that's all right,' said Scanlan, dismounting
from his horse. 'What did she say?'

'She whispered me that she'd slip out and be here in a
few minutes by the short-cut.'

'Good. Now you're quite clear about all the arrange-
ments, aren't you?'

'Oh, make your mind easy, Master John. I've them well
parsed over in my mind. I'll meet you in the morning
with the horse and trap, an hour before day-break, bring
you on here, and then drive the two of ye into Limerick.'

'That's correct, so far as it goes. You have everything
settled about the—marriage; there will be no hitch about
the—clergyman?'

16

'Leave all that to me, Master John,' replied Sullivan. *'I've everything well fixed,'* he added in a low tone.

'I hope you *have,* Sullivan,' said the other, with something of menace in his voice, 'any hitch now, and everything was ruined—Hush!—be off!' he ordered sharply. 'I think I hear her coming.'

Light footsteps approaching blended with the clump of Sullivan's heavy shoes, as he moved rapidly away in the darkness. The sounds faded to silence; and then, out of the darkness, a girl's voice called softly, 'Is that you, John?'

'Ellie, dear!' replied Scanlan, in the same subdued voice, 'who else, but myself.'

The newcomer now came forward, revealing herself in the dim starlight as a young girl of medium height. She placed an agitated hand on Scanlan's arm, with a sound, half sob, half laughter.

'Oh, such a job as I had to slip out,' she said. 'You know, I believe Uncle is getting suspicious.'

'What makes you think so, Ellie?' replied her companion.

'Well, often lately, I've seen him looking at me uneasily, when he thought I didn't notice. Then, a few days ago, he was saying what a heavy responsibility it was on a man to bring up a young girl—that a man could never make up for the loss of a mother.'

'Ah, well, don't worry, Ellie,' said Scanlan, with a note of gay reassurance in his voice. 'Tomorrow, the cat'll be out of the bag, and he'll have no further suspicions—as he'll know the truth.'

'Oh, John!' she said, with a slight tremor in her voice. 'I—I know I should be the happiest girl in all County Limerick—coming to you forever as your wife. But at times, when I think of poor Uncle, and how he loves me, my heart sinks, and I feel—oh, I feel ashamed, and so lonely. Poor Uncle John!' she added wistfully.

As the young girl poured out her heart, Scanlan's body tensed, and there fell a short silence. He was at the youthful age which begets the generous impulse; but if his better nature whispered, 'Beware!' he turned a deaf ear to the warning.

'But, why, Ellie—why?' he said. 'Aren't we going to be married, and won't you have me?'

'Oh, yes, I know, John. You have promised me that

everything will be all right, and I am leaving it all to you. Have patience with your Ellie—she's just a frightened child.'

'But, what's worrying you, Ellie?'

'Oh, just the stealing away from home, without a word of good-bye to poor Uncle who has been so good to me; and then, the secret marriage. Neighbours will talk—they talk for less. It won't be kind talk, and poor Uncle John will have to face it all by himself, and it will be a terrible heartbreak for him.'

'Now, cheer up, Ellie,' said Scanlan, soothingly. 'You know how things are with me. I am only in my twenties, and my people do not take me seriously yet. For the present, I dare not tell them; but everything will come out all right in the end.'

'But, will it, John?—will it? Often when I am thinking —dreaming away to myself, I wonder if your people, with their grand ways, will ever mix with poor Ellie Hanley, the shoemaker's niece. And, even if they *do*, I'll be lost with them. I won't know what to do or what to say.'

'Now, Ellie, put all such thoughts out of your head. When you are my wife, you'll lose all those foolish fears, and you'll drift into our ways, until you are as good as the best.'

'Oh, John, if I could only be *sure*. If I knew that I wouldn't be looked down on because I come from simple, honest country people, how happy I'd be.'

'Put your mind at rest, Ellie,' said Scanlan. 'Remember, no one will look down on *my* wife—I'd like to see who'd do it,' he added defiantly.

'But your people, John?—Do you think you'll get your way with them?'

'I always get my way, Ellie,' he said, with a note of grim humour in his voice. 'But, for the present, we must keep the marriage a secret.'

'I understand, John : you have made it clear. But, will you leave me very much alone when we are married? I'll be very lonely in a strange place, and I'll have no one but you.'

'Have no fear,' he answered. 'You will be quite at home with the woman to whom I am taking you at Glin. We'll be there tomorrow evening, after we are married in Limerick, and, then, you will see me regularly.'

'But what will your people think, John, when you are away so often?'

'Oh, nothing at all, Ellie. Everything is well arranged. I am a regular visitor to Glin, for the shooting and fishing on the Shannon. I've a boat there, and Sullivan comes with me to sail it. You can see my frequent visits there will cause no comment.'

'Oh, John,' she said, in a sudden burst of confidence, 'I'm sure everything will be all right. I trust everything to you.'

'Now, that's talking like a sensible little girl,' said Scanlan. 'Don't forget to be here well before daybreak in the morning. I'll have Sullivan with me, and he'll drive us to Limerick before anybody is astir.'

✽ 4 The Night of the Storm

> Let winds be shrill, let waves roll high,
> I fear not wave nor wind.
> LORD BYRON

THE QUAY OF KILRUSH (the small town on the west side of the Shannon estuary) presented a rather forlorn appearance on the evening of 13th July, 1819. The Limerick boat had left some time since, and as the evening closed in, the skies looked threatening. The only people about were two old boatmen, who lounged against a bollard, puffing pensively at their pipes.

'Looks like a dirty night on the river,' remarked the shorter of the two, as his eye swept the river and the western horizon, where the last red gleams of sunset were being swiftly blotted out by a rolling bank of black clouds.

'I'm afraid you're right, Mick,' said the other, 'and the wind is from a bad point. Look at these black clouds, how they're rolling up.'

'Well, we needn't worry, Garry. We're not putting out a boat to-night.'

'Aye, that's all very well,' said Garry, 'but there's them that must. Look at that boat over there. That's returning to Glin to-night.'

'That's young Scanlan's,' said Mick. 'He came across

this morning from Glin, with his boatman, Sullivan, and a young woman—Hanley, I believe, is her name.'

'They say he's married to her.'

'So 'twould seem; though it's regular robbing the cradle, she's so young.'

'God give you sense, Mick, if you think that would bother Scanlan. He's a wild sort of a devil by all accounts.'

'Ah, well,' said Mick drily, 'the devil a finer cure was ever invented for wildness than marriage. A young fellow may be going round leppin' out of his skin with divarshon; but he isn't long married when 'tis easy to talk to him— Whisht, damn you!' he added suddenly. 'Here are some more Glin people—there's Ellen Walsh in front and three Glin boys in her tail.'

'Hallo, Ellen,' he said, raising his voice, 'where are ye off to?'

'Where do you think?—to New South Wales, maybe,' said Ellen, who appeared to be in high ill-humour, as she came to a stand. 'Tell me, Mick,' she added in a more friendly tone, 'is there any chance under Heaven of a boat over to Glin to-night?'

'Faith, Ellen,' he replied, 'I don't want to have the bad word for you, but I'm afraid it's a blue cuckoo for your chance. Where's the old bawdhoir* who brought ye over?'

'May the devil fry his gizzard!' she said in sudden resentment. 'He says now he won't be able to go back until to-morrow, as he hasn't all his "business" done. Isn't that a nice how-do-ye-do?'

'Hold on, there, Ellen,' said the other boatman, Garry. 'There's young Scanlan's boat. Maybe he'd give ye passage across to Glin—if he's going back to-night.'

'Lord! there's a bit of luck,' said Ellen. 'I thought he'd left long ago.'

'Aye, that's all right; but don't be counting your chickens too soon. How do you know he'll take ye?'

'Don't you bother your head about that, Garry,' she answered. 'Don't I give a hand to young Mrs. Scanlan when she wants help.'

'Oh, that's a horse of another colour,' said Garry. 'Whisht, let ye,' he added hurriedly, 'here's the three of 'em coming.'

As the newcomers arrived, Ellen Walsh elbowed her

* Boatman.

way to the front, with little ceremony, and sidled up to Scanlan.

'Hello, Ellen! what brings *you* here?' he said in some surprise.

'Ah, what, but that dirty blackguard who brought us over this morning, Master John. He's after leaving us in the lurch.'

'H-m. Drunk?'

'No; that'd be a decent thing : but now he tells us that his *"business"* in Kilrush won't be finished till to-morrow —the devil's cure to him. He took good care to keep his ugly clapper shut till he had us stranded here.'

'That was a dirty trick, Ellen. What are you going to do?'

'Well, if I might make so bold, Master John, seeing the fix the blackguard left us in, I was going to ask you to take compassion on us and give us a passage across to Glin. There's me, Pat Case, Jim Mitchell and Jack Mangan.'

'Oh, John,' said the young girl, Ellie Hanley, joining in the conversation, 'if you can manage, we can't refuse Ellen, who has been so very helpful to me.'

'All right, Ellen,' assented Scanlan, 'we'll try to manage you all—though it will overload the boat somewhat.'

'May the blessing of God on you, Master John,' said Ellen Walsh. 'The three Glin boys will be able to give you a hand with the boat—they're well used to the Shannon.'

'That will be all right, Ellen,' he said. 'Now, Sullivan,' he added briskly, 'get all the things on board. The sooner we are off the better, as the tide is near the turn and we'll have a strong ebb against us.'

Scanlan's boat had not made half the journey to Glin, when the threatened storm broke, and the boat with its seven occupants was soon in difficulties. To add to their troubles, a mist was creeping up the river, which made visibility poor, and the strong ebb tide was now against them.

'Shorten sail there, Sullivan,' called Scanlan in a loud sharp voice. 'Do you want to swamp us !'

'If I do, Master John, we'll make no headway at all,' came the reply. 'The tide has turned and is ebbing strong against us.'

'Do as you're told, blast you !' came the angry retort.

'We'll get out the oars to help, and the Glin men will give a hand.'

To this, there was a chorus of assent from the three men, all of whom were at home on the river. Unfortunately, there happened to be only two oars in the boat—a matter that provoked Scanlan to some brief profanity. It was agreed that the two men at the oars would be relieved frequently, as the going against adverse tide was very heavy. In addition, they had to contend with the gale. It was not a head wind : but it was blowing athwart their course and made steering a matter of much difficulty.

'Oh, Ellen,' said Ellie Hanley, who was evidently very frightened at how things were shaping, 'do you think that we're in danger?'

'Now, don't be the least frightened, acushla,' replied the older woman, with a confidence in her voice that she didn't altogether feel. 'All these men are well used to rough weather on the Shannon.'

'But it's so wild, and we have a heavy load on the boat.'

'Ayeah! That's nothing to worry about. Look at me, now—how I'm not frightened,' she added in a bold reassuring tone, for her heart ached with compassion for the young frightened girl, whom she regarded as little more than a child. 'We're as safe as sitting by the fire,' she added as if to settle the matter.

'God bless you, Ellen,' murmured Ellie Hanley, as her hand sought that of Ellen Walsh in a gesture of gratitude. 'You always have the good word.' But even as she spoke, there came a sudden, furious squall, and the boat shipped some water, but not to any dangerous extent.

The young girl shrieked in sudden fright, catching Ellen Walsh by the arm, 'Oh, God have mercy on us—the water is coming in—we're sinking!'

'No! *No!* I tell you,' said Ellen Walsh, vehemently, realising that Ellie Hanley would panic under very little more strain. 'We've only shipped a little water—sure that's nothing at all. Don't be frightened, you poor little darling. I *tell* you we're safe,' she ended firmly.

While the frightened girl trembled on the border line between terror and reassurance, Scanlan's loud, firm voice, raised in command, helped to allay her fear.

'Get the bailer, Sullivan, to that water we've shipped.

Here's a tin for you, Mangan. Now, bail away like hell, the two of you—we haven't shipped very much.'

'There you are now, Mrs. Scanlan,' said Ellen Walsh, soothingly. 'What did *I* tell you? We've only shipped a sup of water over the side. Stephen and Jack Mangan will have it out in no time.'

'Oh, thank God!' said Ellie Hanley. 'I'm so frightened, Ellen. I'm not used to the water like you are.'

'Ah, sure you're only a poor darling of a frightened child,' replied Ellen. 'Now put them little feet of yours up on this old box. Them wisps of shoes you have on you are no better than brown paper for keeping out wet.'

'Oh, Ellen,' said the girl, 'you've a heart as big as a mountain. May God bless you.'

At this point their attention was suddenly diverted by Mitchell singing out, 'Ship's light to starboard.'

'What do you make it, Mitchell?' said Scanlan.

'Very hard to say with the mist; but she's bound for Limerick—There she's in a clear patch, now,' he added. 'A four-master, and bearing a bit nearer to us than I like. Do you think we'll clear her bow, Mr. Scanlan?'

'Not a chance, Mitchell—unless you wish to be run down or capsized. Hell!—she's bearing very close. Back water, men—*hard!*' he shouted to the men at the oars.

'There'll be the hell of a wash from her,' said Mitchell, uneasily. 'She's a big ship.'

'Now, men,' said Scanlan, 'keep the boat's nose into that wash, unless you want us capsized. Sound man,' he added appreciatively to Mitchell—' "The old dog for the hard road." '

The ship was now visible to all in the boat, even through the mist. As she drew level, moving gracefully like a grey phantom, the whole boat's company forgot their own peril for the moment and gazed in awed silence at the passing vessel.

'Oh, Ellen,' said Ellie Hanley in a hushed voice scarcely audible in the wind, 'couldn't we get help from that ship?'

'God bless your head, child. You could bawl as loud as Finn McCool, and they wouldn't hear us with the wind blowing from them.'

'It's very close, Ellen, isn't it?'

'It *is* then,' said Ellen, 'but it's past us now and—

'Oh, my God!' cut in Ellie Hanley, in dire alarm, 'what's happening? Are we sinking?'

'Easy now—easy, pet,' replied the older woman, quickly. 'It's only the wash from that big devil of a ship—I forgot to warn you. There's no danger at all. We'll get a few more heaves, and that's all.'

'Blessed Mother!' said the poor girl. 'Will we ever reach the other side, Ellen?'

'Faith, then, we will—and 'tis you'll have the good laugh when you remember how frightened you were.'

Scanlan, for all his youth, was a boatman of fairly good experience on the Shannon. After another half-hour or so of heavy going against adverse conditions, it was slowly borne in on him that it was next to hopeless to try to reach Glin that night. He decided to test this idea on one of the experienced local men.

'Mangan,' he said, 'you're an old hand on the Shannon. How do you think we're making?'

'Well, Mr. Scanlan, with the mist and the ebb tide, it's not very easy to judge; but we haven't passed Tarbert yet.'

'Do you think we'll make Glin?'

'If we do, we'll be out all night—God save us!'

'Then, there's only one thing to do.'

'I know what's in your mind, Mr. Scanlan.'

'We'll make for Carrigafoyle on the ebb tide—it will be easy going—compared to this, anyway.'

' 'Tis the *only* thing to do, Mr. Scanlan.'

'Very well. Let us alter course. Look! The sky has cleared a bit, and I think there will be no trouble with the steering.'

Carrigafoyle is about ten miles down the Shannon from Glin and on the same side. With the aid of the strong ebb tide, Scanlan's boat, after a difficult and perilous passage, made this haven, despite the storm, and the whole party put up at a house on Carrigafoyle Island for the night. (The 'island' is virtually mainland, from which it is separated only by a very narrow channel).

Early the following morning, Ellen Walsh and the three Glin men left for Glin by road. Scanlan, Sullivan and Ellen Hanley remained behind in Carrigafoyle.

❧ 5 Ellie Hanley Disappears

They sought her baith by bower and ha',
The ladie was no' seen
SCOTTISH BALLAD

THE VILLAGE OF GLIN showed a smiling front on the sunny July morning following that on which the four villagers had walked home from Carrigafoyle. The only reminder of the recent storm was the presence of three thatchers, working within hailing distance of each other, on village roofs, where the wind had held rough revel with the thatched houses.

Ellen Walsh was early astir, looking nothing the worse for her ordeal in the boat, and paused for a moment, as she was about to enter her house, to pass a few words with a neighbour, Grace Scanlan.

'Hello, Grace,' she said, 'you're out fine and early.'

'Would you believe it, I was walking barefoot in the morning dew for my complexion,' said Grace, facetiously adding, 'how are you, Ellen, after your night on the Shannon?'

'Oh, not a feather it took out of me—although, mind you, I've made some rough crossings from Kilrush; but the night before last banged Banagher.'

'You must have been in an awful state, Ellen?'

'Well, no, then. You see, all my attention was on Ellie. The poor child was nearly dead with fright.'

'She's not used to the water. I can imagine how she felt.'

'She's not used to it, indeed, Grace; and I may tell you, a rough Shannon—especially at night, is enough to put the fear o' God into one.'

'Well, ye can be thankful that ye're all to the good. God bless us I thought the wind was going to sweep the roof off the house, and leave the seagulls laughing down at us, in bed.'

'There's a few jobs for the thatchers, anyway, Grace. " 'Tis an ill-wind—" you know.'

'Where did ye leave my namesake and the girl, Ellen. I see no sign of 'em around?'

'Oh, they're behind in Carrigafoyle with Stephen Sullivan.'

'Sh-h-h : they're not. Here are Scanlan and Stephen up the street; but there's no sign of the girl.'

'Hello, Stephen,' said Ellen Walsh, as the two men approached. 'Back again, I see.'

' 'Twould look like it,' said Sullivan, tersely.

'Where's the young missis?'

'Oh, hello, Ellen,' Scanlan cut in. 'We have left her over in Kilrush. She's making a visit there.'

'She'd want a little change, Mr. Scanlan—God bless the child after the awful night she went through.'

'Ah, yes. Not used to the Shannon, like you and your friend Grace there.'

'True for you, indeed.'

'Well, you are none the worse for your experience, Ellen,' said Scanlan, as he moved off, followed by Sullivan.

As the two men moved out of earshot, Ellen Walsh glanced in a puzzled way at her friend, and said in a lowered voice, '*Kilrush!* Did you ever hear the like? Why didn't they leave the poor child there when they *were* there, and not be going see-saw across the Shannon?'

'Oh, there I leave you, Ellen. They're a wild pair—Scanlan and Sullivan.'

'H-m. Like master; like man.'

'Tell me, Ellen : Do you think Scanlan and Ellie Hanley are properly married?'

'Well, now, the thought struck myself a few times; but I'm certain sure Ellie *has no doubt* about it. She's a good girl, and she told me that they were married in Limerick —and hasn't she the ring?'

'Aye, that's right, Ellen; but then what doubts have *you?*'

'Well, for one thing, the way that Stephen Sullivan talks to her—after all he's only Scanlan's hired man.'

'Maybe, it's only in fun. You know Stephen is very friendly with Scanlan—taught him to manage a sailing boat and all that.'

'Listen here to me, Grace. I didn't care that Stephen was Scanlan's foster mother. No man would let his servant show disrespect to his lawful wife. It would be no great harm if Scanlan gave him an odd boot to mend his manners.'

'Ah, well, what's more important is how do you think

Scanlan's people will take the news—when they hear it?'

'I've no doubt in my mind how they'll take it, Grace. There will be proper ructions. *The Scanlans!* Related to the big nobs all over the county.'

'Not a nice look-out for poor Ellie.'

'You may well say—the poor child'

'Well, there's this about it, Ellen. If they're properly married, the Scanlans can draw in their horns. All the high horsing business in the world won't alter *that.*'

Ellen Walsh sighed. 'That's true, Grace, but will they see sense? I think, myself, they'd give Scanlan the long road and the wattle* before they'd let in Ellie Hanley.'

As the weeks passed and Ellen Hanley did not return, gossip was rife in the village of Glin as to where she had gone. For a time Scanlan allayed this gossip by saying that she was staying in Kilrush; later, he stated that she was in Kilkee—the popular seaside resort—with his sister : and, when this came to be disproved, he stated that she had run away with a captain of a ship.

But all speculation was set at rest one afternoon in Glin, about six weeks after the young girl had disappeared.

'D'you think the Limerick boat is in yet?' enquired an old villager from a passer-by.

'It might be,' was the answer. 'You may as well walk down towards the river with me—I'm going that way.'

'No need for me. Here's Jack Mangan coming up.'

'So he is, and he has the devil's own whip under him. I wonder what's all the hurry about.'

'Hey, lads,' called out Mangan, speaking very excitedly. 'Did ye hear the news?'

'What news?' said another villager

'Ellie Scanlan is found!'

'Found,' said the newcomer. 'What do you mean?'

'Ah, is that all the hell *you* know about it?' said Mangan, wrathfully. 'Ellen!' he shouted to Ellen Walsh, who was passing at the other side of the street. 'Ellen Walsh!— Come here—Ellie is found!'

'Glory be to God, Jack,' said the now excited Ellen. 'Where?'

'Across the river—at Moneypoint.'

'Moneypoint? What's she doing there, Jack?'

* Turn him out—a beggar.

27

'Nothing! She's dead—murdered—her body was washed up.'

'God watch over us!' said Ellen, horror stricken. 'What happened? How do you make out she was murdered?'

'It's as plain as the light o' day,' said Mangan, in a voice that quivered with strong emotion. 'She was tied up with a rope—the coroner's jury is after bringing in a verdict of wilful murder against Scanlan and Stephen Sullivan.'

'Oh, God in Heaven, have pity!' said Ellen Walsh, who was very near tears. 'The poor, darling child—who could have the heart to harm her?'

As the news spread rapidly, a crowd gathered around Mangan, seeking for further details. Horror and pity were on every face. In the midst of all the confused talk, a man's voice suddenly rose clear: 'Where are Scanlan and Stephen Sullivan now?'

'Ah! That's what Major Warburton's police would like to know,' said Mangan, as he elbowed his way though the crowd and walked rapidly down the street.

6 *Pursuit*

The master's son, an outlawed man,
Is riding on the hills.
IRISH BALLAD

Scanlan and Sullivan had disappeared. Many weeks had passed since the tragic discovery at Moneypoint, without the slightest trace of the fugitives, although the country for miles around was closely searched by the police, aided by the military.

The high social standing of the Scanlan family in County Limerick, now proved to be a source of acute embarrassment to the authorities. The local magistrates, almost without exception, 'county people,' viewed with the greatest distaste any activity on their part, from motives of delicacy to the feelings of Scanlan's people. As a result, matters more or less drifted, until the authorities decided to call in the services of Major Warburton, Chief of Police in the adjoining County Clare.

Warburton, it may be remarked, was of the type which,

today, would be termed a 'Live Wire.' No social scruples weighed with him where his police work was concerned. He threw himself with energy into the hunt for the fugitives.

Many reports were received of one or other of the wanted men having been seen : but, on investigation, the various reports proved to be valueless.

Then one day in November, 1819, word was conveyed to the authorities that, without possibility of mistake, Scanlan had been seen around his father's place at Ballycahane. Swift action was taken on this report, and in a matter of hours the house was raided by a strong force of police and a troop of lancers. A thorough search was made of both house and grounds, without result. Everything seemed to point to still another wild goose chase, and the search was tailing off.

'Well, sergeant,' said the police Inspector to his glum-looking subordinate, 'any luck?'

'Not a trace, sir. We've searched every cranny from ground to roof.'

'Another false alarm, I fear. Damn those country people with their cock-and-bull stories.'

'I suppose I'd better call off the men, sir?'

'Just as well, sergeant. No use wasting any more time.'

While the foregoing conversation was in progress downstairs, two lancers were completing the search of a loft over the stables. Like the police Inspector, they were of the opinion that they had been engaged on a fool's errand.

'I'm fed up with this job,' grumbled the taller of the two, as he carefully fingered his head, which he had bumped against a cross-beam in the half-light. 'What say, Ginger?'

'Same here, chum,' was the reply. 'This is no job for us, chaps. Nurse-maiding old Warburton's police around the country. Why can't they do their own police work without having us leading them by the hand?'

'If 'twas some bloke stole a few hens, Ginger, he'd have been caught long ago; but what—Hello!' he exclaimed, as the shrill blast of a whistle broke in on his plaint, 'hunt is off.'

'About time,' said Ginger in evident relief. 'Let us hop

it, chum. Nothing in this damn loft but cobwebs.'

As the two lancers made for the steps leading to the
stables underneath, Ginger's companion suddenly paused.
'Hey,' he said, thoughtfully. 'Did we search that pile of
straw in the corner?'

'Must have,' said the other. 'Give it a poke of your
toothpick, just for luck,' he added.

The lancer to whom this suggestion was made, raised
his lance and plunged it carelessly into the pile of straw,
saying, facetiously, 'Hop out of it, chum—I see you!'

The sequel was startling. There was a muffled yell from
the pile—a sudden upheaval of the straw—and out stag-
gered John Scanlan, pale and shaken. He had very nearly
been transfixed by the casual thrust of the soldier's lance.

Pandemonium broke out. While one lancer ran to the
head of the step-ladder, and yelled excitedly to those below,
the other, with poised lance, stood guard over Scanlan,
shouting to him not to stir. The order was unnecessary.
Scanlan, standing dazed and shaken after his narrow escape from death, was in no mood for flight.

The chase was over. Within the hour, John Scanlan, the
young, sporting squire, whose gay smile had fluttered many
a heart, was on his way to Limerick prison under heavy
guard, to stand trial, 'before God and his country' for the
murder of his reputed bride of two weeks.

7 On Rumour's Wing

> To hear an open slander is a curse!
> But not to find an answer is a worse.
> OVID

ALTHOUGH DECEMBER WAS STILL YOUNG, the first breath of
frost had etched its fairy tracery on the window of Doctor
McCullough's breakfast room in the little town of Bruff.
Outside, the shrubs glittered in a fleeting beauty, soon to
be dissipated by the morning sun. From the chimneys of
the nearby houses, the smoke curled lazily in the still air.
Winter, like a good salesman making his first contact, had
spread out a choice sample of his stock-in-trade.

The doctor stood hands in pockets and back to the fire,

his eyes fixed on the window. At a casual glance it might seem that he was enjoying the beauty of the out-of-door; but closer inspection would reveal his gaze fixed on vacancy. Now and then, a heavy frown puckered his forehead. He shifted his feet uneasily and sighed. From this reverie he was aroused by a light step in the passage outside, and turned to see his wife enter the room.

'Hullo, Betty,' he said, 'how do you like the way the youngster is looking this morning?'

'Oh, fine, David,' she answered. 'He is almost quite himself again.'

'Just as I told you last night he would be. The little beggar was suffering from nothing worse than an overdose of sweetcake.'

'Yes; I think you're right, David. I'm afraid I'm over anxious about our children. By the way,' she added, looking at him searchingly, 'are you feeling all right yourself? You look tired and worried.'

'Oh, it's nothing at all, Betty,' he replied. 'Just a little bit off colour—it will pass off.'

'You are worrying—you are worrying for me, David?' She paused, and then added in a halting tone, 'You are worrying—worrying about—John!'

'And if I am, Betty, dear Heaven, haven't I cause?' he answered, drawing his finger tips wearily across his forehead. 'Look at the trouble and disgrace into which he has plunged innocent people. *You* are wilting under the strain, although you do your best to keep up a brave front. I'm not blind—do you think that doesn't wring my heart; and think of our little children—branded by your brother's misdeeds. They little know what lies before them.'

As David McCullough ceased, his wife advanced timidly, and laid a hand that trembled slightly on her husband's arm. 'David,' she whispered, 'don't give way to bitterness. It is hard—it is very hard on you, and that is not the least of my worries. But, there is one of these worries which I must drag out in the open—anything is better than the suspense.' Her voice trailed away under the stress of emotion. She paused, and then, recovering herself somewhat, added : 'David, you must give me an answer to this question, which has been gnawing at my heart since the dreadful news of John's arrest. *Has it changed you to me? Are* things different between us now? Do not fear to speak out your mind—it would be a mistaken kindness to hide it from me. The truth would be far easier to bear than the doubt.'

As Elizabeth McCullough was speaking, the troubled look in her husband's eyes faded and gave place to one of tender compassion. Clasping a hand gently around each of her shoulders, he said : 'Betty, dear, we have enough of trouble in this house without adding to it by an imaginary one. I do not visit the misdeeds of your brother on your innocent head. If anything your distress has only drawn you closer to me. That is the bare truth.'

'Oh, thank God,' she faltered. 'Thank God for that mercy. At least one of my crosses has been removed. I didn't know—I thought—Oh, I thought you were sick of the whole Scanlan family, and the thought was getting me down.'

'Make your mind easy about that, Betty,' he answered. 'But that doesn't mean that my feelings towards your brother are anything but bitter resentment for the disgrace he has brought on us all.'

'David,' she said in a supplicating tone, 'David, dear, aren't you a little less than just to condemn John in advance. He may be wild and wayward; but I cannot—I cannot believe that he is guilty of this cruel murder of the young Hanley girl.'

'I hope time—and the jury—will prove you're right, Betty,' replied her husband, moodily. 'God knows I have no wish to add to your worries; but it would be better to look facts in the face than to build up a house of cards which the first breath of evidence in court may blow down.'

'That is not so certain, David. They are sparing no effort at home in John's defence. Daniel O'Connell has been engaged—they say he seldom loses a case. But, apart from that—I know you do not share my view, I believe John is innocent; and God will not allow the innocent to suffer.'

As Elizabeth McCullough pleaded her brother's cause, her husband grew more and more ill at ease. He was torn between two emotions : on the one hand, love for his wife, and anxiety to lessen her worry; and, on the other hand, with conviction of her brother's guilt. John Scanlan, although his brother-in-law, he regarded as an unqualified blackguard; but in this bitter opinion he was probably influenced by the fact that there was open hostility between himself and Scanlan's father, against whom he had taken an unsuccessful lawsuit over some money matter. Up to a comparatively recent date, Dr. McCullough had been serving as an Assistant Surgeon in the British Army, but, after the failure of his lawsuit, he lost his commission, and the blame for this he laid at his father-in-law's door, alleging that the elder Scanlan had written a defamatory letter about him to his Commanding Officer, in connection with the lawsuit.

The uncomfortable trend of the conversation was relieved for the doctor by the entrance of a maid, who announced that a neighbouring gentleman had called to see him.

'Rather early for a call, Betty,' said the doctor to his wife. 'I'd better see what he wants. Show him in here,' he added to the maid; 'I don't suppose there's a fire in the drawingroom.' Mrs. McCullough slipped quietly out of the room, and left her husband alone to meet his visitor.

'Hullo, Dick,' the doctor greeted, as a well set up man of middle age, with a pleasant expression, entered the room. 'What brings you out so early—your old friend, sciatica?'

'No, David,' replied the other. 'I never felt better; though whether that's due to your ministrations is a moot point. Can I have a word with you, undisturbed?' he added, dropping his light tone.

'Why, certainly,' replied McCullough, glancing at his friend enquiringly. 'We're all right here.'

The newcomer paused, then walked over to the fire, extending his palms to the blaze, while the doctor watched him curiously. After a rather long pause, the visitor wheeled suddenly around and faced the doctor.

'Damn it all, David,' he burst out; 'this is a rotten errand for me.'

'What on earth is the matter?' said McCullough, in surprise. 'I can't imagine a careful old stager like you in any trouble.'

'It's not myself,' was the reply. 'Nothing at all to do with me. *You're* the one concerned.'

McCullough gazed at his friend in some astonishment, and then said, impatiently, 'Oh, for Heaven's sake, Dick, let's have no more of this mystery. In plain language, what the devil have you got on your mind?'

'It's about John Scanlan,' said the now flustered Dick.

'There's a rumour going around—it's in everybody's mouth almost, that it was you laid the information which led to his arrest. This rumour must be nailed at all costs, David, or it will do you no end of damage. Think of your position as a medical man. I hate having to tell you all this; but I would fail you as an old friend if I kept silent while the mischief spread.'

While the speaker was delivering his distasteful news, an angry flush spread over Dr. McCullough's face. When his friend ceased, the doctor remained silent for a short space, staring into the fire and then burst out: 'God in Heaven! this is the last straw. As if the disgrace piled on my innocent wife and children were not enough, now my personal character is the target for mud slinging. Who, in God's name, can have started this?'

'Calm yourself, David,' said his friend. 'Take it easy, old boy. As to who started the rumour, was it ever found who started any rumour? Possibly some wretched busy-body remembered that you were not on good terms with your people-in-law, and speculated that you might have been trying to even things up with them.'

'Damnation,' said the now thoroughly exasperated doctor, 'this will ruin me, and I am powerless to stop it. But there must be some way. It's *got* to be stopped. Can't you think of something, Dick?' he added, rather pathetically.

'Well, there's only one effective way that I know of,' replied the other, 'and I've been racking my brains on how to nail this damn lie. Write to Dublin Castle and ask the authorities to issue a denial. That would be only bare justice on their part, and it would clear your name effectively.'

This solution appealed to the doctor as a heaven-sent inspiration, and he acted on it without delay. Unfortunately, he wrote the letter while smarting under the first flush of anger, and, instead of presenting his request in temperate language, he lashed out at his people-in-law, whom he accused of starting the rumour. His brother-in-law, John Scanlan, came in for the brunt of the attack, although it was obvious that Scanlan, who was in gaol at the time, awaiting his trial, could have had nothing to do with it.

There can be no doubt that Dr. McCullough had nothing whatever to do with John Scanlan's arrest, as can be seen from McCullough's letter to the Castle. This is further borne out by the letter of Henry Lyons, the Croom magistrate, who mentions the handing over of ten pounds received from the authorities, for the man who gave the information. The smallness of the reward clearly indicates that this man was some casual opportunist.

8 The Trial

Man, false man, smiling destructive man
NATHANIEL LEE

The trial of John Scanlan, for the murder of Ellen Hanley, the 'Colleen Bawn,' opened at the Limerick Spring Assizes, in mid-March, 1820, the presiding Judge being The Honourable Richard Jebb, 4th Justice of the King's Bench.

The courthouse in which the trial was held stands opposite the historic St. Mary's Cathedral in Bridge Street. The building is still in a good state of repair, but has been converted into schools run by the teaching order of the Irish Christian Brothers. In this connection it is interesting to note that Gerald Griffin, whose well-known novel, *The Collegians,* is a fiction version of the Colleen Bawn story, himself became a Christian Brother and his bust now adorns the front of the schools where, as a young reporter, he attended the trial of Scanlan.

The trial created an extraordinary interest among the citizens of Limerick and people living in adjoining counties, and for weeks before and after the trial it was the general topic of conversation. This was partly owing to the high social standing of the Scanlan family, and partly owing to the extreme youth of the two principal actors in the tragedy. The 'Colleen Bawn' was not quite sixteen years of age : Scanlan was in his twenties.

No effort was spared in the prisoner's defence. Scanlan's people engaged as Counsel the celebrated Irish lawyer, Daniel O'Connell, whose fame as a lawyer extended far beyond his own shores.

While there was no tendency to underestimate the danger in which Scanlan stood, it was felt by his people that, with O'Connell at his back, he would be acquitted. No doubt they were sustained in this opinion by a firm belief in Scanlan's innocence. It was true that he had earned the reputation of being impetuous and wild; but—and it was a big but—it was a long shout from mere 'wildness' to murder.

His people's optimism must have affected Scanlan, for, on the day of his trial, he entered the dock with a confident step, and glanced around the court without the slightest trace of fear.

'Hats off! Silence in Court!'

At the familiar order from the court crier, the loud buzz of conversation in the body of the court gave place to dead silence, broken only by a brief, shuffling noise as the people rose to their feet on the entrance of the Judge.

On the order, 'Put forward John Scanlan,' the prisoner stepped briskly to the front of the dock, and the Clerk of the Crown, in his level, impersonal voice, read out the indictment :

John Scanlan, you stand charged that on or about the 14th July, 1819, in collusion with another, not yet in custody, you did kill and murder one Ellen Hanley, otherwise Ellen Scanlan, your reputed wife, against peace and statute of our Lord the King. Do you plead guilty or not guilty to the charge?

To this, Scanlan replied, in a clear, firm voice, 'Not Guilty,' and the jury having been sworn, the Prosecuting Counsel, Mr. Pennefather, proceeded to open the case for the Crown :

'Gentlemen of the Jury: it falls to me, as prosecuting Counsel for the Crown, to place before you, as clearly and as briefly as possible, a summary of the evidence which will be submitted for your consideration by the prosecution.

'The evidence to be submitted is not that of an eye-witness—or witnesses. It is, however, a clear case of circumstantial evidence, which, if established before you, points, the prosecution submits, to the clear guilt of the prisoner, beyond any reasonable doubt.

'There is a tendency among some people to decry circumstantial evidence, to look upon it as little better than mere suspicion, on which it would be unthinkable to find any accused guilty. It would be hard to find a more mistaken attitude. Circumstantial evidence is not only legal and fair; but often it may be relied on to a far greater degree than the actual evidence of a single eye-witness.

'A single eye-witness, through no fault of his own, may be unreliable in his testimony as to what he observed. He may have been labouring under a strong excitement at the time of the occurrence, and, gentlemen, you all know how that may warp a man's power of observation. On the other hand, he may have some strong bias, one way or the other, as to the innocence or guilt of the prisoner, and, as a consequence, his evidence may be warped by his prejudice—even without his knowing it. But a chain of facts, established by several witnesses, all pointing to the same conclusion, cannot be affected by personal prejudice or hasty observation, and must be regarded as of equal weight —indeed I would say, of greater weight, than the direct evidence of a single eye-witness.

'But, whether the evidence be simple, direct evidence, or circumstantial evidence, it is the solemn duty of the jury to the prisoner, to weigh every particle of the evidence with the most scrupulous care, and if, as a result of this painstaking examination of the evidence, you find that it does not point convincingly to the prisoner's guilt; if you entertain a reasonable doubt—and by reasonable doubt, I mean such a doubt as would enter your mind if you were dealing with an everyday business matter of your own : if you entertain such a doubt on examination of the evidence, then, gentlemen, your clear duty is to give the prisoner the benefit of it, and return a verdict of "Not Guilty."

'If, on the other hand, you find that all the evidence leads you to only one possible conclusion, and that conclusion, the guilt of the prisoner, beyond any reasonable shadow of doubt, then, gentlemen, it is your duty to return a verdict of "Guilty"—without regard to the consequences, for these are not your responsibility. But, in your deliberations, remember that the Prosecution is not out to strain evidence against the prisoner. . . . The Law seeks justice—not blind vengeance.

'I shall now proceed to a brief review of the case on which you will shortly be deliberating.

'The prisoner, John Scanlan, a young man of good education and upbringing, belonging to a respected family of high social standing in County Limerick, made the acquaintance of Ellen Hanley, as near as can be gathered, towards the end of 1818, or early in the following year. He may, indeed, have known her in a general way much earlier, as his home was only a short distance from where she resided with her uncle.

'Ellen Hanley was the daughter of a farmer : her mother was dead, and she had been adopted by an uncle, one John Connery, who resides in Ballycahane, not far from the home of the prisoner, John Scanlan.

'Now, gentlemen of the jury, it requires no strong effort of the imagination to appreciate the ease with which this young country girl—she was not quite sixteen years of age —fell under the spell of a young gallant like Scanlan, with his polished manners and gay appearance. But—and I would like to emphasise this point, though Ellen Hanley may have been the child of parents of scanty means, she was a girl of unblemished character, and there is no question that—so far as she knew—her association with Scanlan was never other than a strictly honourable one.

'Towards the end of June, 1819, Scanlan, who may then have been genuinely in love with the young girl, prevailed on her to elope with him, and they went through a form of marriage—a secret marriage—in Limerick. There is good reason to doubt the validity of this marriage; but, on one aspect of it there can be no doubt, whatever. Ellen Hanley firmly believed that the marriage was a valid one, and that she was John Scanlan's lawful wife.

'Immediately after the marriage, Scanlan took her to live in Glin, a village, as you are aware, on the east side of the Shannon, about eight miles below Foynes. This locality was not a haphazard choice. For a considerable time Scanlan had been in the habit of making excursions to the village, for the fishing and shooting on the Shannon. In consequence, his absence there would arouse no suspicions among his people at home in Ballycahane—the very last thing in the world which he desired.

'Scanlan had not been long living in Glin, when, the

Prosecution submits, his position began to dawn on him, and he began to see himself in a situation in which he would be held up to the censure of his own people and the ridicule of his friends; a situation in which he found himself encumbered with a peasant girl, to whom he may—or may not—have been legally married, but who stood not an earthly chance of being admitted to the inner circle of his aristocratic friends, and Scanlan's infatuation began to wane—to wane rapidly. Within a fortnight of the so-called marriage, Ellen Hanley was no longer his chief joy, but his chief problem. Scanlan's reputation—even among his friends—was that of a wild, impetuous young man. . . . . The stage was set for tragedy!

'We now come to the 13th July, 1819. On the evening of that day, Scanlan, Ellen Hanley, and the boatman, Stephen Sullivan, were returning by boat from Kilrush, on the opposite side of the Shannon to Glin. At Kilrush quay, Scanlan was accosted by four Glin people whose boatman had disappointed them and these people succeeded in inducing him to give them a passage across the river to Glin. During that passage, they were overtaken by a violent storm, as a result of which they had to put in at Carrigafoyle, some eight miles or so down the river from Glin, but on the same side, where they remained for the night.

'In the morning, the Glin people continued their journey home by road, the last to leave being Ellen Walsh, who will testify that, as she left Carrigafoyle, she saw the prisoner, John Scanlan, Ellen Hanley, and Scanlan's boatman, Stephen Sullivan, together . . . . *That was the last that was seen of Ellen Hanley alive.* Her next appearance in this tragic story is when her body was washed ashore at Moneypoint, on the Clare side of the Shannon, some seven weeks later.'

The Crown Prosecutor then reviewed the evidence to be tendered by the witnesses whose testimony follows : the first witness called for the prosecution was Ellen Walsh.

A good deal of importance was attached to the evidence of this witness, so much so, that it had been suggested that she should be sent to Dublin during the long waiting interval before Scanlan's trial. Situated in the more or less isolated village of Glin, the authorities feared that she would be influenced by friends of the Scanlan family in the matter of her evidence. In the result, however, this fear proved quite groundless.

Mr. Pennefather, opening the examination of Ellen Walsh :

'You remember the night of the 13th July, last year?'

'I do, indeed.'

'Will you tell the jury why you remember it so positively.'

'Wasn't it the night we were all nearly drowned, crossing from Kilrush to Glin.'

'In what circumstances did you make that crossing?'

'Well, there was me, and Jack Mangan, Pat Case and Jim Mitchell went across to Kilrush in the morning and, when we were ready to go home in th' evening, the old blackguard of a boatman, who brought us over from Glin, wasn't ready to go back until the next morning.'

'U-m; I see. What happened then?'

'Well, as luck would have it, Lieutenant Scanlan, with young Mrs. Scanlan, and Steve Sullivan, their boatman, were going back to Glin, and I palavered Lieutenant Scanlan to give us passage across.'

'I understand you had a rough crossing?'

' "Rough!" Huh. Rough's no name for it. What between the heavy storm and the ebb tide, we had no chance of making Glin, and we had to put in at Carrigafoyle for the night—or what was left of the night.'

'You all spent the night together at Carrigafoyle?'

'We did.'

'And what happened in the morning?'

'Well, the three men from Glin left by road as soon as it was light, and I followed after them a little later on.'

'Whom did you leave behind you in Carrigafoyle?'

'I left Lieutenant Scanlan, young Mrs. Scanlan, and Steve Sullivan.'

'When did you next see any of these three people?'

'On the morning after that, Lieutenant Scanlan and Steve Sullivan came in to Glin.'

'Were you speaking to them on their arrival?'

'I was.'

'Did you make any enquiries for young Mrs. Scanlan?'

'I did. I asked Steve Sullivan where she was.'

'What did he say?'

'Well, Lieutenant Scanlan answered for him and said they had left her in Kilrush on a visit.'

'Did it strike you as strange that young Mrs. Scanlan should go back on a visit to a town which she had only just left?'

To this question, the prisoner's counsel, Daniel O'Connell, objected, on the grounds that the idle speculation of a witness was not evidence. This objection was upheld by the Judge, and the Prosecuting Counsel changed the form of the question:

'Well, I'll put it to you in this way: To your knowledge, when was Ellen Hanley last in Kilrush?'.

This question appeared to Ellen Walsh, who was not versed in the subtleties of the law, as a foolish one, for she answered with surprise, 'Only the day before, of course, isn't that plain?'

This answer in no way abashed Mr. Pennefather, who continued:

'Now you saw Lieutenant Scanlan and Stephen Sullivan in Glin on the morning following that on which you left Carrigafoyle . . . . *When did you next see young Mrs. Scanlan?*'

'Oh, God between us and all harm—the poor darling—about seven weeks later.'

'Where did you see her then?'

'At Moneypoint, on the other side of the river, where her body was washed up.'

'You went over to identify her?'

'No. I didn't. The magistrate—the Knight of Glin—took me over, as I knew her. so well.'

'Had you any difficulty in identifying the body as that of young Mrs. Scanlan?'

'No. I knew her beyond any doubt whatever. I couldn't be mistaken in her front teeth.'

'Will you please explain to the jury why you had no doubt in the identification.'

'Well, the poor child had a double tooth at each side of her face. There was no mistaking them—they were odd.'

At this point the Crown Prosecutor motioned to the Court Crier to bring forward a large parcel, which, on being opened, revealed a quantity of feminine apparel. The articles were spread out for exhibition, and the examination of the witness continued:

'Now, I want you to scrutinise carefully some women's garments which will be exhibited to you, so that you may tell the jury if you have ever seen any or all of them before—Hold them up, please,' he added to the Crier.

Ellen Walsh scrutinised the garments carefully. 'Yes,' she said. 'Grey mantle—frock—skirt—two silk spencers. Yes. I know them all.'

'Do you know the owner?'

'Yes. They belonged to young Mrs. Scanlan.'

'You have no doubt of that?'

'Oh, none whatever. They were in her small round trunk the night in Carrigafoyle. She was showing us all the nice things she had while we were waiting for daybreak.'

'When did you see them next?'

'About a week after. I saw some of them with Steve Sullivan's sister, Maura, and a neighbour, Grace Scanlan, had one of the yellow silk spencers and the skirt.'

This concluded the direct examination of Ellen Walsh, and Daniel O'Connell took up the cross-examination.

'You say that you identified the body washed ashore at Moneypoint, after long immersion in the water, by certain double teeth?'

'I did.'

'Now, you must be well aware that double teeth are fairly common. How can you swear positively to these particular teeth?' O'Connell paused, and added sternly— *'Remember, a man is on trial for his life.'*

Ellen Walsh returned O'Connell's stare without the least trace of uneasiness, and answered with some heat : 'Do you think I'd have it on my conscience if there was any chance of mistake. These teeth were very odd. I can swear to them beyond any manner of doubt, whatever.'

'You knew young Mrs. Scanlan very well?'

'I did, indeed. I was a help with her for a bit when she came to Glin.'

'During the time you were helping Mrs. Scanlan, how did she get on with Lieutenant Scanlan—as far as you observed?'

'Oh, the poor child was light about him—there's no doubt about that.'

'You mean she was devoted to him?'

'Isn't that what I said?' replied the witness in some surprise.

'Now, what about Lieutenant Scanlan?' pursued O'Connell.

'Oh, I'd say he was a bit gone on her, too; but, you know, Mr. O'Connell, a man doesn't show his feelings like a poor ownshuck* of a woman would.' (Laughter in court).

'No. I suppose not,' replied O'Connell, dryly. 'From your observation, however, was Lieutenant Scanlan attached to his wife?'

'Oh, I'd say he was so. He gave her a lot of nice presents of one kind or another.'

This concluded Ellen Walsh's testimony.

The next witness called was Maura Sullivan, who stated, in reply to a query from Prosecuting Counsel, that she was a sister of Stephen Sullivan (Scanlan's boatman).

'You see this grey mantle, which was found in your possession,' continued Mr. Pennefather. 'In what circumstances did you come by it?'

'I got it from my brother, Stephen.'

'The mantle, as you can see, is an expensive garment. Is your brother in the habit of making you costly presents?'

'Indeed, then, he isn't.'

'Did you ask him where he got it?'

'Well, I did; and he said he bought it.'

'From where, exactly, did he produce this expensive mantle, which he—*bought* for you?'

'He took it out of a small, round trunk, in the possession of Lieutenant Scanlan.'

'Did you ever see that trunk before?'

'I think it was young Mrs. Scanlan's, and Ellen Walsh told me it was the one she saw with her the night at Carrigafoyle.'

'Did you get any other articles of dress out of this trunk?'

'I did. Lieutenant Scanlan gave me a pair of shoes, a pocket book, a cap, and a ribbon out of the same trunk.'

'You didn't ask him where he got them?'

'No, indeed. I knew my place better than that.'

'Was it a common occurrence for Lieutenant Scanlan

* A half-wit woman.

and your brother to make presents of women's attire when they came to Glin?'

'Indeed, then, it wasn't. That was the first time I ever saw women's wearables with them.'

'Now, on the occasion that Lieutenant Scanlan and your brother were scattering presents of women's garments, did you notice anything new or unusual about themselves?'

'My brother, Stephen, was wearing a plain, gold ring, and Lieutenant Scanlan had a figured gold ring on him— a "keeper," you know, which I never noticed before.'

'Did you ask your brother where he got the plain, gold ring?'

At this question, Maura Sullivan paused, looked warily at the Crown Prosecutor, and, finally answered, 'No.'

'You knew young Mrs. Scanlan quite well, I take it?'

'Oh, yes; I knew her well.'

'When Lieutenant Scanlan and your brother returned without her, did you make enquiries for her?'

'I did. I asked Lieutenant Scanlan where she was, and he said she had gone to Kilrush on a visit.'

'Was that the only occasion on which you enquired for her?'

'I asked for her again about a week after, and Lieutenant Scanlan told me she was in Kilkee with his sister.'

'Did anything happen later on which reminded you of this statement?'

'There did. Lieutenant Scanlan sent me with a letter to his home in Ballycahane, and when I came back, I told him that I saw his sister, Miss Scanlan, but I didn't see young Mrs. Scanlan.'

'What did he say to that?'

'He said that she had made off with the captain of a ship, and that was why I didn't see her.'

This concluded Maura Sullivan's direct examination. O'Connell decided not to cross-examine; but stated to the Judge that he would like to recall the witness, Ellen Walsh, with reference to her identification of the trunk out of which Maura Sullivan was given the women's apparel.

On her recall, Ellen Walsh swore that the trunk in question was the one which she had seen with young Mrs. Scanlan on the boat and at Carrigafoyle.

Mrs. Grace Scanlan was the next witness called by the Prosecution. She stated that she was no relation, whatever, to the prisoner, John Scanlan. The Crown Prosecutor then produced for her inspection a number of women's garments.

'Do you recognise any or all of these articles of women's attire?'

The witness scanned each article carefully : 'Silk spencer —yes; and the sprigged skirt—yes, I know that; the silk handkerchief—I know that, too. Yes; I know the lot of them.'

'They were found in your possession. Where did you obtain them?'

'From Stephen Sullivan.'

'Where had he these articles when he handed them to you?'

'He took them out of a trunk with a round lid.'

'Did you ask him where he got them?'

'No : I understood that they were young Mrs. Scanlan's.'

'And you accepted from Stephen Sullivan without any comment, wearing apparel which belonged to Mrs. Scanlan?'

'*No. I did not,*' said the witness sharply, flushing with resentment. 'I said to Lieutenant Scanlan, who was there at the time, that I was surprised that he allowed Stephen Sullivan to make so free with the clothes—what right had he to give them away.'

'A very proper remark,' commented the Crown Prosecutor. 'What did Lieutenant Scanlan say in reply?'

'He said that it was all right—that she had made off with the captain of a ship.'

'Yes; that put things straight for you, as regards accepting the garments.'

'It did so, or I'd have nothing to say to them.'

'Now, tell me, Mrs. Scanlan—take your time, and think carefully—did you notice anything unusual about Lieutenant Scanlan or Stephen Sullivan on the occasion in question?'

'In what way?'

'Well, anything unusual in what they were wearing.'

'Um—well, no, I don't think—Oh, wait a minute. They both were wearing gold rings, which I never noticed on them before. Stephen Sullivan's was a plain gold wedding ring; but Lieutenant Scanlan's was a keeper ring—'twas figured.'

'Did you ask them where they got the rings?'

'Oh, Lord, no. My answer mightn't be too polite.'

Grace Scanlan's evidence having concluded, she was not cross-examined, and the next witness, John King, was called.

The witness, tanned from exposure to the weather, and bearing the typical appearance of a seafaring man, took his place on the witness stand and glanced calmly around the court, with complete self-possession. In reply to the opening question of Crown Prosecutor, as to his occupation, he replied, 'Well, I make out, mainly, with my boats.'

'Now, you see this rope in my hand,' continued the Crown Prosecutor. 'I want you to examine it very carefully—take your time—and tell the jury if you ever saw it before.'

King examined the rope, carefully. 'Yes,' he said, 'it's my own rope, without a doubt.'

'You are quite certain of that?'

'Oh, no doubt in life; it's my own rope.'

'In what circumstances did this rope leave your possession?'

'Well, coming on to the middle of last July, I met Lieutenant Scanlan in Glin, and he asked me for the loan of a rope, as he was going for a sail on the Shannon.'

'And you identify this rope as the one you gave him?'

'I do, without a doubt.'

'When and where did you next see this rope?'

'About seven weeks later, at Moneypoint, on the Clare side of the Shannon.'

'Will you tell the jury the circumstances which led to the finding of the rope.'

'Well, when the body of young Mrs. Scanlan was washed up at Moneypoint, the magistrate and his party engaged me to take them over from Glin; and, when we got to where the body was————.'

'Yes, continue, please.'

'Well, you could have knocked me down with a straw when I saw the poor girl's body trussed up with my own rope.' (Sensation in court, and excited, low conversation, which was quickly suppressed by the court crier.)

This concluded John King's direct examination, but Daniel O'Connell, for the defence, took up his cross-examination:

'You say that you lent this rope to Lieutenant Scanlan in Glin, coming on towards the middle of July last?'

'Yes; that is correct. His boatman, Stephen Sullivan, was with him at the time.'

'Now, I presume you are a busy man, fully employed with your boats?'

'Well, fairly. I don't complain.'

'Now, I put it to you that it is quite possible that Lieutenant Scanlan returned this rope within a reasonable time; but that the matter escaped your memory in the press of other matters?'

'No; that's wrong, Mr. O'Connell. I'm sorry to contradict you.'

'Oh, don't mind that, John. You should hear what some of my learned brethren say to me at times. (Laughter in court.) Now, why are you so positive that Lieutenant Scanlan did not give you back the rope?'

'Well, as the time was passing, and I saw no sign of it coming back, it started giving me a bit of a heart-scald; for 'twas a good rope, and I did not want anyone to stick to it.'

'Well, letting that pass, you agree with me, don't you, that ropes look mostly alike?'

'Oh, I wouldn't say that, Mr. O'Connell. They might to a landsman; but they wouldn't to a boatman.'

'But how can you say, *positively,* that this is your rope. Couldn't it be a rope very like it?'

'Do you see that splice there on the rope?' said King, catching up the rope again, and indicating the splice with his finger. 'Well, that splice was made *with my own two hands.* I could swear to that splice if it came from the bottom of the Red Sea.'

This concluded King's evidence, and the next witness called was John Connery, the uncle of the murdered girl.

There were general murmurs of sympathy as this witness took his place on the stand, a sympathy that was shared by all, as was evident from the sympathetic tone of the Crown Prosecutor's voice in opening the examination.

'What is your relationship to the deceased girl?'

'I'm her uncle. I brought her up since she was six or seven years of age, when her poor mother—a sister of mine—died.'

'Will you tell the jury the circumstances in which she left your house?'

'Well, at the time that she eloped with Mr. Scanlan, she was only about fifteen years of age. She was a very pretty girl; but I never suspected anything until Tuesday, 29th June, last year, when she disappeared. There was no trace of her when I called her.'

'Was there anything missing from the house?'

'Ah, she took £100 in notes and twelve guineas in gold, and I never heard trace of her after that until about six weeks later, when I heard that she was dead.'

'Your life's savings. All gone!'

'Ah, don't blame her, sir; she was very young and my sister's child. The loss of the money might be got over; but who can give me back my little girl!'

'No one is blaming her, Mr. Connery. She was very young, as you say, and probably thought the money had been saved up for herself. Now, I'll not distress you further than one more question—for we all feel deeply sorry for you—had the young girl any marks or peculiarities by which she might be distinguished?'

'She had two double teeth in her upper gums; one on each side of her face.'

This witness was not cross-examined, and the Knight of Glin, a magistrate for County Limerick, was next called.

This witness stated that he was a magistrate for the County Limerick, and, on hearing of the finding of the body at Moneypoint, he crossed from Glin immediately, taking with him Major Odell, and Ellen Walsh of Glin. On reaching the Clare side of the river, they were joined by Major Warburton, head of the police force in that county.

While crossing the river from Glin, Ellen Walsh gave him a detailed description of the deceased girl, and described the clothes she wore. Previous to viewing the body, Ellen Walsh also mentioned to him that he would notice two projecting teeth in the upper gums—one at each side of the face—if the body were that of the missing woman.

Witness went on to detail how he swore an inquest, at which the testimony of Ellen Walsh was taken, previous to the body being taken up from the place where it had been temporarily interred on the strand by two fishermen.

When the body was disinterred, it revealed that a rope had been tied tightly around the neck. The sockets of the projecting teeth were also plainly visible, although the actual teeth were missing from the sockets. The body of the poor girl was in a bad way. One arm was missing and a leg was broken. A remnant of a bodice was found on the strand.

Ellen Walsh had described the deceased's clothes already, and witness continued that he got some of these with Mrs. Grace Scanlan, with whom Mr. Scanlan lodged. The mantle he got with Maura Sullivan, whom he arrested.

At this point the Knight of Glin identified the various articles of clothing and the rope with which deceased was bound. The clothes answered in every particular to the description which Ellen Walsh had furnished of the garments beforehand.

Asked by the Crown Prosecutor what steps he had taken when the inquest returned a verdict of wilful murder against Scanlan and Sullivan, the Knight of Glin stated that he had returned immediately to Glin with the intention of arresting both of the men, but found that they had disappeared. An energetic pursuit was kept up until it became hopeless. Thereafter, when any information was received as to the whereabouts of either of the men, steps were taken immediately to test its accuracy. All the reports received were founded on baseless rumour, or else the information was so stale as to be useless.

This concluded the Knight of Glin's evidence, and, after some minor witnesses had been examined, the case for the Prosecution closed.

No witnesses were called for the defence, and Daniel O'Connell rose to address the jury on behalf of the prisoner, John Scanlan.

'Gentlemen of the Jury: You have heard the learned Counsel for the Prosecution warn you that the Law seeks not blind vengeance but justice.

'In the case which you are now about to consider, that warning is peculiarly opportune; for who, contemplating the tragic end of this innocent and lovely young girl, can feel anything in his heart but burning indignation against her ruthless destroyer.

'But, gentlemen, no matter what indignation you may feel—an indignation shared by us all—no matter how you may wish and pray that the wretch who snapped the thread of Ellen Hanley's young life may be brought to justice, you must not let that indignation blind your judgment; you must not for a single moment forget that the law of the land regards the prisoner at the bar as an innocent man, unless, and until, he is proved guilty by evidence so clear and convincing as to leave no reasonable doubt in your mind as to his guilt. Let no feelings, therefore, of righteous anger against the perpetrator of this callous crime, bias your judgment when considering the case. Your duty lies in a dispassionate sifting of the evidence placed before you in this court, and into that sifting, no emotion may enter other than a solemn desire to hold the scales of Justice fairly as between the prisoner and the Law.

'I would earnestly impress on you, in particular, the solemn obligation of dismissing from your minds any gossip or comments which you may have heard outside of this court; any opinion or comment which you may have heard as to the prisoner's guilt—or, for that matter, his innocence.

'John Scanlan has now been under detention for the past four months, and, from our knowledge of human nature, it is too much to expect that he has not already been tried not once but many times by the amateur lawyers and judges of the country cottage and city club. Gentlemen of the Jury, if you do not want to be false to your oath, you will put all such uninformed pre-judgments resolutely out of your mind, and confine yourself, strictly, to the legal evidence which has been tendered in this court.

'The Prosecution seeks to prove that the prisoner who now stands before you, is guilty of the atrocious murder of his young and lovely wife, within a few brief weeks of their marriage, and they ask you to believe that the impelling motive to this dreadful crime lay in the anticipated disapproval of his people, when the fact of the marriage became public.

'Now, gentlemen, there stands before you the prisoner, John Scanlan, a young man—a very young man, of good family, good education, and good upbringing. Young as he is, he has already seen service as a lieutenant in the Royal Marines, where habits of discipline and restraint formed an essential part of his training.

'In his civil life, it is common knowledge that Scanlan's

recreations lay, mainly, in the manly, out-of-door sphere—shooting, fishing, and sailing on the Shannon. By upbringing, by training, and by his own choice of the manly out-of-door life, therefore, you have all the ingredients that go to make up the gay and generous nature, which endears its possessor not only to friends but to acquaintances.

'Is this the type of man who would descend to the murder of a young and trusting wife? and for no greater reason, according to the Prosecution, than that his parents might not approve of his marriage. Gentlemen, cast about in your own experience of human nature, and ask yourselves if the crime is not fantastically out of proportion to the alleged motive. Who would hang a dog on this far-fetched theory?

'It has been suggested by the Prosecution that Scanlan was not legally married to Ellen Hanley—that the marriage, in fact, was a bogus one. Very well; let us take them at their word and see where the suggestion leads us.

'If Scanlan was not legally married to Ellen Hanley, as the Prosecution suggests, then the whole case against him collapses for want of motive. There is no longer any necessity for him to worry about the social penalties for having married beneath him. To use a homely phrase, "We weren't born to-day, nor yesterday," and we know quite well that in the social circles in which Scanlan moves, his deception of a young peasant girl would incur no greater penalty than a mild "tut-tut" here and there: the slight lifting of an aristocratic eyebrow; or a playful reference, perhaps, to "our young Don Juan"—an epithet which may be almost regarded as a compliment in view of the popularity which Byron—in his person and writings, enjoys in the select circles.

'Going on the Prosecution's suggestion that the marriage was a bogus one, where is now the powerful, compelling motive to induce the prisoner to stake on one cast of the dice, the happiness and good name of his people, his own reputation, and not only his reputation, *but his life?* . . . Gentlemen of the Jury, you will see for yourselves that such a motive did not exist.

'But, you may well ask yourselves, if John Scanlan is innocent of this young girl's murder, then *who* committed the crime; for it is not contested—indeed in the circumstances, it could not possibly be contested—that Ellen Hanley was murdered. Well, gentlemen, I shall submit to you a theory which bears not only the stamp of possibility, but of extreme probability; a theory which will not do violence to your sense of reasoned judgment—as I submit the Prosecution's theory does—and which fits in in every particular with the evidence which you are about to consider.

'John Scanlan had in his employment a boatman and general servant, named Stephen Sullivan. Now, it is well known that this Stephen Sullivan was something more than a mere servant by Scanlan. Sullivan invariably accompanied him on his shooting and fishing trips on the Shannon. He had taught Scanlan how to handle a sailing boat, and he had been his tutor in other outdoor pastimes. From their constant association out-of-doors, the relation between them was a free and easy one. Scanlan never treated Sullivan as a servant, and Sullivan, on his part, was obsessed with a dog-like devotion to his young master; a devotion which brooked no obstacle in his master's way, and which made him quite ready to strike down anybody who crossed that master's path.

'Here, gentlemen, I submit, is the signpost which clearly points the road leading to the murderer of Ellen Hanley— or, if you will, Ellen Scanlan. You have this fanatical follower nursing the conviction that his young master and friend, having married beneath him, is faced with social ruin. Sullivan has no illusions as to the attitude of the social circle in which Scanlan moves to a peasant-girl wife. He is well aware that on every hand his master will be faced with embarrassment and half-concealed ridicule, and—he is equally well aware that Scanlan knows this to be the case.

'Every frown that now crosses his master's face, Sullivan attributes to the predicament in which Scanlan finds himself with Ellen Hanley. Every sharp word from his master, which before would pass unnoticed, Sullivan lays against Ellen Hanley's account. He sees her as the one who has placed John Scanlan in an impossible position, as the rock which has cleft the happy stream of his young master's life, and . . . he determines to take the remedy into his own hands, and, without breathing a word of his fell purpose, to blast that rock out of his way.

'Gentlemen of the Jury: does not the logic of what I have suggested strike home to you? If I am wrong, *why has Sullivan disappeared?* Why is he at the present moment a fugitive from justice? To that query, reason and commonsense can give but one answer: Find Sullivan and you find the murderer.'

As O'Connell proceeded with his speech for the defence, it became evident that he was making a profound impression on the jury, and, if they had retired to consider the case at the conclusion of his speech, it is more than likely that John Scanlan would have been acquitted.

Counsel for the Prosecution followed, however, with a trenchant reply, pointing out, among other matters, that if the fact of his being a fugitive proved Sullivan guilty, the test applied with equal force to Scanlan, who had been a fugitive for four months.

The Judge summed up and the jury retired. After a fairly lengthy absence, they returned with the announcement that they could not agree. The Judge then asked them to retire again and give the case further consideration.

The jury had now been absent for some time, and tension was mounting in the crowded court. In the place allotted to the public, people were gathered in small knots, eagerly discussing in low voices, the chances for and against the prisoner.

'They're inside a long time, aren't they?' said a powerfully built man, bearing the definite impress of the country, and probably from the prisoner's neighbourhood. He wiped his face with a large handkerchief, although the day was anything but warm, and stared fixedly at the door leading to the jury-room.

'Aye. They are, that,' replied his friend; 'but you can't blame them. I wouldn't like to be serving on this trial.'

'I thought that Dan had got him off,' said the first speaker.

'So he would, only for old Pennefather coming after him. However, the disagreement looks well for Scanlan.'

'Huh! There are two ways of looking at that. Some of them think him guilty, anyway—Whisht!' he added, quickly, 'I believe they're coming out.'

'Hats off! Silence in Court!'

As the familiar order rang out, the jury filed back to their box and the Judge took his place on the bench. All eyes were fixed on the returned jury, whose inscrutable faces gave nothing away of the fateful decision to which they had come. There was a dead silence, in which the gentle rustle of some papers sounded loud and harsh, when the Clerk of the Crown spoke:

'Gentlemen of the Jury, have you agreed on your verdict?'
'We have,' replied the foreman.
'Do you find the prisoner at the bar guilty or not guilty?'
We find him guilty of murder!
There was a sort of muffled gasp from the public in court. A lady was heard to moan in stricken tones, 'Oh, my God!' General whispering and shuffling of feet were quickly suppressed by the court crier, and the Clerk of the Crown again addressed the prisoner, who, alone, preserved the same serene calm he had exhibited throughout his trial.

'John Scanlan, have you anything to say why sentence should not be passed on you according to law?'

Scanlan turned his gaze on the judge, and then slowly swept it around the court, as if inviting the earnest attention of those present to what he was about to say. Speaking in a clear, firm voice, which betrayed neither emotion nor fear, he said:

May the gates of Paradise be ever shut against me if I had hand, act, or part in the crime for which I am now about to suffer. If Sullivan be found, my innocence will appear.

There was a pause, broken only by a woman's sob, and then the Judge addressed the prisoner:

'John Scanlan, I do not intend that any words of mine should add further pain to the dreadful position in which you now find yourself. It only remains for me to pass on you the sentence prescribed by law for the crime you have committed.

'You shall be removed from the place where you stand to the gaol whence you came, and on the 16th March, 1820, you shall be taken thence to the common place of execution, where you shall be hanged by the neck until you are dead, and your body given to the surgeons of the County Hospital for dissection; and may the Lord have mercy upon your soul.'

During, and after the passing of the sentence, the prisoner kept a completely firm demeanour. He half-turned, smiled rather wistfully to somebody in the court, and left the dock with a firm step, in charge of his guard.

The verdict came as a stunning shock to Scanlan's friends and family, as it had been confidently expected that he would be acquitted. Couriers rode through County Limerick immediately, obtaining signatures from many influential people, praying for a respite. To all pleadings for mercy, however, the Judge refused to listen.

⚜ 9 *The Curtain Falls*

> Then black despair,
> The shadow of a starless night, was thrown
> Over the world in which I moved alone
> PERCY BYSSHE SHELLEY

THURSDAY, 16th MARCH, 1820. An unusually large number of people are abroad in the streets of Limerick. In the vicinity of Ballsbridge large crowds have collected, and all eyes are fixed on the northern, or Clare, side of the bridge.

At this period the Limerick gaol was situated in that part of the city known as 'The Island.'

The place of execution for convicts was not, strange to say, within the precincts of the gaol, but on Gallows Green, on the outskirts of the city, approximately a mile distant from the gaol. On this Gallows Green public executions were carried out in full view of all who cared to attend the utterly barbarous spectacle. It need scarcely be added that the practice of public executions was, at the time, general everywhere.

To go from the gaol to Gallows Green it was, of course, necessary to cross the river (by Ballsbridge), and here the waiting crowds craned their necks for the first glimpse of the carriage in which Scanlan would be conveyed.

'The whole of Limerick seems to be in the streets to-day,' remarked a spectator to his friend.

'Small wonder,' replied the other. 'People have talked of nothing else since the trial started.'

'Do you think he's innocent?'

'My God! I hope not—although it's a queer thing to

say. But 'tis an awful thought—an innocent man going to his doom!'

'Aye, or a guilty man, for that matter. However, if he's guilty, he deserves it.'

'"If" . . . .I'd like to see it beyond any doubt. He's very young, and they say he was a good sportsman,' he added, rather inconsequentially.

'Aye; so they say; and you seldom see a sportsman with a bad streak in him.'

' 'Twas a pity they couldn't nab Sullivan. A lot of people think that he's the man who did it.'

"They'll get him, sooner or later; but that won't be much use to Scanlan if he's proved innocent when he's under the sod.—Hullo! What's up now?'

From the vicinity of the bridge had arisen the clamour of excited voices. Soon, above the din, could be heard shouts of 'Here he is!' 'They're coming!' and other cries that clearly indicated that the prisoner, with his escort, was approaching. Suddenly, the clamour increased; there was a loud command, 'Halt!' and the mounted escort came to a stop.

'What's up, young fellow?' demanded an old grandfather with a blackthorn stick, of a young lad who was perched on a wall to get a better view. 'What's up?' the old man repeated, giving the boy a poke of the stick to attract attention.

'The carriage horses won't cross the bridge,' replied the boy excitedly.

'What the hell do you mean, "Won't cross the bridge"?' retorted the old man, catching some of the excitement.

'They won't cross the bridge, I tell you,' said the boy. 'Isn't that plain?—Oh, Look! Look!' he added, 'there's a soldier prodding 'em with the point of his bay'net.'

'That'll soon move 'em on,' said the old chap, grimly.

'No! no!' shouted the boy, in rising excitement. 'The horses won't budge. They won't cross the bridge!'

By this time the clamour had swelled to an immense volume.

'My God! that's queer,' muttered the old man. Women shrieked, and high above the din another woman's voice sobbed in hysterical excitement:

It's the hand of God!—He's innocent!'

The refusal of the horses drawing Scanlan's carriage to

Gallows Green, to cross the bridge over the river, is authenticated from several reliable sources, and is beyond question. It made a deep impression on the crowds; and, many who before were ready to condemn Scanlan, saw in this incident an omen of his innocence. As is well known, it is easy, at times, to sway the feelings of a crowd, and when Scanlan jumped alertly from the carriage, and walked with head erect on the long journey to Gallows Green, there was a complete swing-over, in his favour, of the attitude of the onlookers. Loud murmurs of sympathy could be heard on all sides, coupled with such remarks as, 'Oh, what a pity; he's so young,' 'Why didn't they wait till they caught Sullivan?' 'Who can say he isn't innocent?'

But whatever could be said at the time as to Scanlan's innocence or guilt, it could be said with certainty in his favour that throughout his ordeal, he preserved a rare courage, and died, protesting his complete innocence of the crime.

Months passed, and the sensation of the 'Colleen Bawn' tragedy was fading; fading so far as the man in the street was concerned.

In the meantime, however, nothing, in a sense, had been settled. Two schools of thought now arose; the one, holding that Scanlan had been unjustly condemned; and the other, contending the he deserved his fate. There was one thing, and one thing, alone, which would resolve this problem : *Find Sullivan, and bring him to trial!*

10 The Stranger in Scartaglen

Thus let me live, unseen, unknown,
Thus, unlamented, let me die
ALEXANDER POPE

THE TWILIGHT OF THE LONG MAY evening was mingled with the early moonlight in Scartaglen, Co. Kerry, as John Fitz-Gerald completed the trimming of the oil lamp in his bar parlour, and lit up for the night. Two customers present watched the operation with the intentness of people who have nothing to do, and all the evening to do it.

'That's better, Mr. Fitz,' observed one of the men. 'Makes things more homely. It's good for trade, too,' he added with a grin. 'I can see now that my friend Clifford's pint is nearly empty. Finish up that and have another.'

'No—no. It's my turn to stand,' said Clifford. 'Two pints, Mr. Fitz—and blow the tops off 'em. Don't give us half froth, warm weather or no.'

'Keep a civil tongue in your head, Clifford,' said the publican, bridling at the jest. 'If you don't like what you're getting here, there's an outside and an inside to my shop door—and you can pick whichever pleases you.'

'There you are,' said Clifford, derisively, to his friend. 'Nice way to talk to one of the people who're keeping the roof over his head.'

'He has his money made,' said the friend sententiously.

'Be damned to that! Who made it for him but the likes of you and me?' He fell silent a moment, and, suddenly burst into rather discordant song:

> I went into an inn where I met an acquaintance
> I took a few drinks and I paid what I owed—

'That's enough of that, Clifford,' called out the publican, sharply. 'No singing in this house.'

'Ah, have a heart, Mr. Fitz. What am I doing out of the way? Just a few bars of a song to lift up a man's heart.'

'Well, you'll have to lift it with something else,' was the reply. 'I won't have my place turned into a cheap jig-house—Here!' he added, in a tone of annoyance, 'haven't you anything smaller than a note to pay for the porter?'

'Only a few coppers, Mr. Fitz—unless you'd like to chalk it up to me.'

'Oh, I think I have the change,' said the publican, dryly, as he counted it on to the counter. 'That's the second note I've changed for you this week. You must have been left a legacy.'

'Well, the wife's old man didn't hand her over to me empty-handed.'

'H-m,' commented the publican, glancing at Clifford with something like pity. 'And wouldn't you, like a decent man, go home to the young wife you married only a few weeks ago, instead of sky-highing her money although I say that against myself,' he added, with a wry grin.

'Maybe you're giving me good advice, Mr. Fitz,' said Clifford, after a moody pause. 'But a few pints sometimes helps a man to forget.'

'Four weeks married!' said the publican, in an enquiring tone, 'and you're talking about forgetting. Tell me! Is this a case of the girl I left behind me?'

Clifford started slightly, looked sharply at the publican, and then muttered slowly : 'Maybe it is—and, maybe it isn't.' He paused, and then, with false heartiness, added, 'Ah, I was only fooling—Good night, Mr. Fitz!' saying which, he put down his pint measure abruptly on the counter, and walked out of the shop.

'Damn queer chap, that friend Clifford of yours,' remarked the publican, to the remaining customer. 'He's gone and left half his pint unfinished. What do you make of him?'

'Now, you've got me, Mr. Fitz,' said the other. 'He keeps his mind to himself. Nobody is quite sure where he came from, or how he made his living before he came to Scartaglen. One minute he's full of life, and the next, the devil wouldn't drag a word out of him—his mind is up in the clouds. A queer chap, as you say.'

'Nice way for a newly married man to be getting on. The wife's father is fairly comfortable, I believe?'

'Aye. So I believe. He's employed on the Brandon estate.'

'Oh, well,' said the publican, dismissing the matter, 'we've enough of worries of our own, without bothering about Clifford and his cranky ways.'

A day or two after the conversation in FitzGerald's public house, the villagers of Scartaglen had their curiosity tickled by the appearance of two well-dressed strangers in the village. A little spice was added to the event by the fact that they were accompanied by the police sergeant from Castleisland, some five miles distant.

One of the newcomers was seen to call at a number of shops in the village, before strolling into the licensed premises of John FitzGerald.

'Good day to you, friend,' said the visitor pleasantly to the publican, who was leaning in a restful attitude across his counter, customers being few so early in the day.

'Good day to you, sir,' replied FitzGerald. 'This will make another scorcher of a day. The crows will have their tongues out.'

'How's the porter?' queried the visitor.

'Oh, in the finest of condition. I keep the wet sack over the barrel in this weather—nothing to beat the wet sack on the hot days,' he added, knowingly, with the air of a man betraying a trade secret.

'Good man. Draw me a sample, will you.'

There was a swish, as the publican placed the pint measure under the tap, which would sound as sweet music to any thirsty traveller, and FitzGerald placed the drink on the counter, with the remark : 'There you are—as good as you'll get in County Kerry.'

'Thanks,' said the stranger. 'By the way,' he added, 'do you mind changing a fiver for me? I'm a bit short of change.'

'Oh, that will be quite all right, sir. I think I can manage it,' said the publican reaching for a canister on the shelf at his back, from which he produced some banknotes. 'One—two—three—four—just a minute now, and I'll get you the odd silver from the till. . . . There you are, sir. I think you'll find that all right. Ah, good-day to you, sergeant,' he added to a police sergeant who had just entered the shop. 'You don't often visit us these times. I suppose the police in Castleisland think we're all saints in this village,' he added, jocularly.

'Sergeant !' said the stranger, sharply.

'Yes, sir,' said the sergeant, coming smartly to attention.

'While I call my assistant, you will keep Mr. FitzGerald

under observation. He is not to leave the shop,' saying which, the stranger left suddenly.

'What the hell alive is this about?' bawled FitzGerald, 'and who is that spawn o' hell who orders me not to leave my own shop?'

'Easy! easy! Mr. FitzGerald,' said the sergeant soothingly. 'He's a high police officer from Dublin, here on special business.'

'I don't care a hell he was the Lord Lieutenant,' said the publican in a furious rage. 'No man will order *me* about in my own house.'

'Whisht, Mr. Fitz, for the Lord's sake,' implored the Sergeant, who was obviously ill at ease and puzzled. 'It may be all a mistake—whisht!' he added, 'here they're back.'

The stranger now returned in company with the man who had been seen around the village with him earlier. 'I must ask you to remain where you are, Mr. FitzGerald,' he said in a courteous but firm voice, 'while my assistant searches your house.'

'Search *my* house!' roared FitzGerald, now thoroughly aroused. 'What the hell for?'

'You have been found in possession of forged bank-notes. Two of the forged notes you gave me in change a moment ago are forgeries.'

' "Forgeries!"—forgeries, you say! Well, if they are, I've been swindled myself. The sergeant there can tell you that I'm an honest man.'

'That may very well be; but possession of forged bank-notes, you will admit, is a very serious matter that requires investigation. Where did you get them?' he added sharply.

'Well, I had only the four notes, in all—all the other money was in silver,' said FitzGerald, calming down somewhat at the other's even tone. 'Two of the notes I got from a man named Clifford; the other two I got from an honest old farmer, who paid me a bill.'

A search of FitzGerald's house revealed no further bank-notes. The publican and Clifford were, however, placed under arrest. The publican, well-known as an honest trader, was bailed out immediately; but Clifford, who had come to the locality only recently, was lodged in Tralee gaol, on a charge of uttering forged bank-notes.

11 Denounced

> I could a tale unfold, whose lightest word
> Would harrow up they soul
> WILLIAM SHAKESPEARE

LATE ONE EVENING, about a week after the incident of the bank-notes, a sturdy country-man, named Dillon, might be seen walking briskly up the drive of Kilrudery, the residence of the Knight of Kerry.

Arriving at the main entrance, he beat a sharp summons on the knocker, and fidgeted impatiently with the toe of his shoe in the gravel while waiting for a reply. The door opened, revealing a young, and rather pompous looking footman, who gazed at Dillon's serviceable tweeds.

'Aw. What do you want, my man?' he said. 'Are you not aware that this is not the tradesmen's entrance?'

' "Aw" to yourself,' replied Dillon, coolly. 'A tradesman wouldn't be calling at this hour of the evening. Is the Knight inside?'

'The Knight of Kerry is in residence.'

'Well, tell him Dillon is here, like a good boy.'

'What is your business?'

'My business with the Knight is urgent and no concern of yours. I gev you your message—didn't I?'

'Stand in here, my good man, and wipe your shoes.'

'If you don't hurry up, I'll wipe one of them in the back of that fancy breeches of yours.'

The footman, feeling that relations were getting rather strained, made his way to the Knight of Kerry, without further comment, and announced that there was a man at the door who wished to see the Knight on urgent business, adding, 'A rather aggressive person, Sir; says his name is Dillon, and that his business is both urgent and confidential.'

'Dillon?—Dillon?' said the Knight. 'Now who—Oh yes, Jenkins, that is all right; show him in.'

'Will you come this way, please,' said Jenkins, on his return to the waiting Dillon, who treated the footman to a derisive wink, and commented, 'That's better, me lad!'

When Dillon entered the room where the Knight of

Kerry was seated, he gave a sharp, backward glance, to see that the footman had retired, and then bent a keen glance on the Knight, to see how he was taking the intrusion.

'Good evening, Dillon,' said the latter. 'I was leaving for Valentia when you called recently, and had no time. What's all the row about that you want to see me so urgently?'

'You'll excuse me for bothering you, Knight, when you hear the news I have for you.' He paused, to add force to what he was about to say, and added, in a lowered voice : *'I've found Sullivan!'*

At this the Knight of Kerry swung round and stared at Dillon with sharp interest. *'Sullivan!'* he said after a short pause. 'Do you mean the man wanted for the Shannon murder?'

'The very man, Knight. I've him safe and sound, where he won't get out of in a hurry.'

'Where !'

'In Tralee gaol.'

'What sort of nonsense are you talking, Dillon,' said the Knight, with some impatience. 'How could *you* commit a man to gaol?'

'Well, it's like this, Knight. I was landed in the gaol myself for a couple of days, on a charge of desertion, until they found out their mistake (the devil take 'em,' he growled in an angry undertone) 'and the second day I was there, who did I spot in the prisoners exercising in the yard but my bould Sullivan.'

'Quite impossible, Dillon. I would have heard of his arrest, immediately.'

'Asking your pardon, Knight, but you wouldn't. You see he's not there in his own name. They don't know him as Sullivan in the gaol.'

'What do you mean?'

'He has a false name now. He calls himself Clifford.'

'But what is he doing in the gaol?'

'He was took up for passing bad bank-notes on Fitz-Gerald, the publican, in Scartaglen.'

'Ah-h ! so *that's* the fellow. This information is very important, Dillon—if it is correct. You are quite sure of your man?'

'Oh, the devil knock me blind as a bat, Knight, if

there's any mistake. I'd know his hat on a hedge.'

'Is he aware that you identified him?'

'I took good care of that. The minute I spotted him, I dodged out of the way, and then went on a sick—moryah, so that he wouldn't knock across me.'

'Very well, Dillon. I'll look into the matter, at once; and if your information is correct, I'll recommend your action to the authorities.'

The Knight of Kerry lost no time in testing Dillon's information, and its accuracy may be seen from the following letter, dated 18th May, 1820, sent by The Right Hon. Maurice FitzGerald, Knight of Kerry, to Under Secretary Gregory, Dublin Castle:

Dear Gregory,

I have committed to Tralee Goal, Stephen Sullivan, the associate with Scanlan (executed at the last Limerick Assizes) in the horrid murder on the Shannon.

He had concealed himself in this county for some time past, under a false name. The fellow who informed me, executed the business capitally, and deserves any reward which belongs to the discovery.

12 Sullivan's Trial

How happy is he born or taught,
That serveth not another's will.
SIR HENRY WILSON

Over twelve months had elapsed since the murder of Ellen Hanley, the 'Colleen Bawn,' had horrified the country, before Stephen Sullivan appeared in the dock of Bridge Street courthouse, Limerick, to stand his trial for the crime.

The case, which was heard on the 25th July, 1820, attracted almost as much attention as the trial of John Scanlan on the same charge, a few months earlier.

One reason for this interest was the argument of the well-known lawyer, Daniel O'Connell, at the Scanlan trial, that Sullivan, alone, had plotted and carried out the murder, under a crazy obsession that Ellen Hanley had spelt social ruin for his young master.

In happier times, Scanlan—a gay and impetuous young man—had many friends, as his type always has. These friends carefully fostered the theory that Scanlan had died an innocent man and that the *real*—and only—culprit was his boatman, Sullivan. Their efforts to clear their friend's name were aided by Scanlan's courageous bearing throughout the trial, and by the unusual courage he had shown, in walking, unaided, to the place of execution when the horses refused to cross the river.

The trial of Sullivan—it was hoped—would resolve all doubts as to Scanlan's innocence. If O'Connell's line of defence proved to have been well-founded, it would bring a qualified happiness to every relative and friend of Scanlan. It would not, indeed, restore the life which the Law had declared forfeit—but, what was almost as desirable, it would restore Scanlan's good name, and erase the stain of conviction for a cruel murder.

Public excitement and speculation were at a high pitch, therefore, when Stephen Sullivan stepped into the dock, to stand trial for his life, as the legal formula then had it : 'before God and his country.' As a contemporary account puts it, 'The court was crowded to excess by persons of the first respectability, to hear the development of a murder so mysterious in its perpetration.'

Messrs. Quinn, Pennefather and White, instructed by Matthew Barrington, Crown Solicitor, were for the Crown. The prisoner, Sullivan, was not legally represented. When the judge had taken his seat, the Clerk of the Crown read out the indictment :

Stephen Sullivan, hold up your right hand. You stand here indicted for, that on or about the 14th July, 1819, you, not having the fear of God before your eyes, did wilfully, felon- iously, and of your malice prepense, kill and murder Ellen Hanley, otherwise Ellen Scanlan, against peace and statute of our Lord, the King. How plead you? Guilty or Not Guilty?

To this, Sullivan replied, 'Not Guilty,' and the jury having been sworn, Mr. Counsellor Quinn, who led for the Prosecution, rose to address the Court :

'My Lord, and Gentlemen of the Jury : The prisoner, Stephen Sullivan, stands charged with one of the blackest and most hideous murders that has, perhaps, ever stained the annals of criminal jurisdiction.

'You are well apprised that the shocking transaction which is the subject of the present trial, has been already publicly discussed in court, and that one unfortunate person, charged with the commission of the crime, after conviction upon the clearest and most indubitable evidence, has made atonement by the deserved forfeiture of his life to the offended laws of justice and humanity.

'In the course of that trial, the name of the prisoner at the bar was frequently mentioned. Much of rumour, and, indeed, of direct imputation of his being an accomplice in the guilt, existed there, and has continued since; *but*, it is my duty to observe, and I am persuaded your own sense of duty has already anticipated, that, notwithstanding such rumours and imputations, the prisoner stands at this moment as unaffected as if that trial had never taken place, or as if his name had never been mentioned until the present hour; and, allow me to assure you that, atrocious and singular as the case is—almost beyond example, I should have waived my right as Counsel for the Crown of prefacing the evidence with any statement, but that, in a case confessedly circumstantial, it appeared to me essential towards a perfect understanding of the facts that ground the charge.

'Gentlemen, that this unhappy young creature, Ellen Hanley, was murdered, no rational doubt whatever can be entertained. Her body, identified as it will be to you, by the same evidence which furnished most satisfactory proof to a former court and jury, was thrown ashore from the Shannon, in a state demonstrating the violent torture of her death. One arm and one leg were broken; she was tied neck and heels, and almost devoid of clothing, with a rope pressed so tightly around her throat as to manifest strangulation.

'Before this unfortunate girl had attained her sixteenth year, she was seduced from the protection of her uncle, with whom she had lived from her infancy. She decamped suddenly from his house, taking with her one hundred pounds in notes, and twelve guineas in gold—all that the wretched man was worth in the world; and both her person and the plunder she brought with her became the preconcerted spoil of the wretched man who has been executed, and of the prisoner at the bar, who appeared as his servant, and was, certainly, his associate.

'It will appear that on the 13th July, 1819, Scanlan purchased a boat, and that on the evening of that day, there embarked in that boat at Kilrush, apparently proposing to proceed to Glin, the persons I shall mention, namely : Scanlan, Sullivan (the prisoner), Ellen Hanley, the deceased, a girl of the name of Ellen Walsh—who will be produced, and three men of the names of Case, Mangan and Mitchell.

'In the boat was a trunk belonging to the deceased girl containing various articles of women's dress beyond her condition in life, and very remarkable in their description. The boat, meeting with adverse weather conditions and an ebb tide, was unable to make the journey to Glin, and had to take shelter at Carrigafoyle, where the party landed at an advanced hour, and passed the remainder of the night there, at the house of a woman named Ellen Walsh —not to be confused with the other Ellen Walsh, of Glin, who arrived with the party in the boat. In the morning, the three men, Case, Mangan and Mitchell, left by road for Glin, and never joined the others of the party again.

'At this house in Carrigafoyle, which belongs to Mrs. Walsh who will be produced, Ellen Hanley opened her trunk to display her finery to Ellen Walsh of Glin, who had crossed in the boat with her. In this manner the Glin woman, Walsh, became perfectly acquainted with the articles of dress, and will identify them during the trial.

'The period to which I now wish to direct your attention is most important, and the fact I am about to state, of vital consequence in the case. In the morning, after the three men had left for Glin, the boat pushed off across the narrow channel, with Scanlan, Sullivan, Ellen Hanley, the deceased, Ellen Walsh of Glin, and no others.

'Having been put across the channel, Ellen Walsh proceeded on foot to Glin, and the boat proceeded out on the Shannon, which is very wide at this point, *with no persons in her save Scanlan, Sullivan, and the deceased.* From that time, Ellen Hanley was never seen alive

'The girl, having disappeared, questions were, naturally, asked of those who had been seen last with her. To those questions, the prisoner gave contradictory accounts, from their nature utterly irreconcilable with innocence. On one occasion, he said that they had shipped her off with an American captain on the Shannon; on another, that she had gone to Scanlan's sister at the seaside town of Kilkee in County Clare. In addition to this, these articles of dress, identified as they will be, were traced, and will be proved to have been in the possession of the prisoner, and sold and disposed of by him.

'Gentlemen, the facts which compose this circumstantial case will incontrovertibly appear—circumstances indisputably established in point of fact, frequently bring more sound conviction to the human mind than direct and positive testimony, subject, as it is, to error and deception.

'It is your consolation that they are open to explanation. If they can be satisfactorily answered on the part of the prisoner, he will be entitled to your acquittal. If they cannot . . . I think they will appear to you as irresistibly conclusive of guilt; and, if such is the case, you will consign him without regret to that fate which the laws of God and man pronounced upon the—Murderer.'

When Counsel for the Prosecution had concluded his opening address to the jury, the Judge turned to Sullivan and asked him if he had any Counsel employed for his defence. To this query the prisoner replied : 'I have no money to fee Counsel or Attorney, my Lord, and have nobody to look to but you and the Great God to give fair play for my life.'

The calling of the witnesses for the Prosecution then began; but, as the evidence tendered in the case of Stephen Sullivan differs in no important detail from the evidence given at Scanlan's trial, and, as not a single witness appeared for the defence, we pass on to the Judge's charge to the Jury, at the conclusion of the evidence.

The learned Judge began his charge by directing the attention of the Jury to the important parts of the evidence.

'But', he said, 'before you proceed to your deliberations there is one point on which I would more particularly direct your attention, and that is, whether the dead body which had been found on the strand by the fishermen, was that of the young woman who was left in the boat at the time Ellen Walsh saw the three sail off together, and which young woman was never afterwards seen.'

To direct the jury as to this fact, he recapitulated the evidence of Ellen Walsh of Glin, the first witness, who stated that two projecting teeth were in the upper gums of deceased; but, on viewing the body, the teeth were not visible; but the sockets or holes were there.

'The fisherman who first discovered the body,' continued the Judge, 'stated that the two projecting teeth were in the mouth when he found the body. Here there is a variation between these two witnesses; but the testimony of Ellen Walsh was confirmed by the Knight of Glin, a gentleman whose rank in life, and the extreme prudence and caution with which he proceeded in this case, makes his evidence of great importance.

'He examined the mouth of the deceased, and pointed out to the inquest the holes in which the teeth were. Besides, the clothes described to him by Ellen Walsh, when found by him, answered minutely to her description of them.'

His Lordship then alluded to the variance of the prisoner at the bar and his master, as to how they disposed of the girl, the prisoner saying that she had gone off with a captain or officer, the master that she was at his sister's in Kilkee. 'This variation was of much importance, and yet the prisoner does not produce any evidence as to where the young woman went, although it is twelve months since the murder was committed. It was also of consequence the prisoner having women's clothes in his possession, and offering them for sale to Mrs. Scanlan, the lodging woman.'

His Lordship then pointed out the nature of circumstantial evidence, as being more clear and conclusive than any other, and concluded, after many observations on the enormity of the crime. He implored the Jury to give the evidence mature deliberation.

The Jury, having retired, returned in about a quarter of an hour. Immediately, there was a dead silence in the court, as the Clerk of the Crown put the usual question :

'Gentlemen of the Jury, have you agreed upon your verdict?'

'We have.'

'Do you find the prisoner at the bar guilty or not guilty?'

'We find him guilty of wilful murder!'

The verdict caused no surprise among the spectators in court. Unlike the Scanlan case, where O'Connell's eloquence had maintained the element of doubt up to the last, the people seemed to have made up their minds on what the jury's verdict would be in Sullivan's case, at the conclusion of the evidence. All eyes were turned on the unfortunate man in the dock, as the Judge proceeded to address him, before passing sentence :

'Stephen Sullivan, you have been found guilty upon evidence that has not left a particle of doubt in the mind of anyone who has heard your trial. You have been found guilty of a crime, the most diabolical that could be committed.

'The Law obliges me to pass upon you its awful sentence. The Law obliges me to do so, that those who have heard your trial may also hear your sentence. It is unnecessary for me to dwell upon the enormity of the offence of which you have been found guilty. There is not one present possessed of a human heart, but must shudder and recoil at the barbarous and bloody deed. You have taken away the life of an innocent fellow-creature . . . a child, I may say. For the commission of this diabolical crime, you received no provocation; but you have been the willing instrument in gratifying the lust of your wretched master.

'You have now but a short time left you in this world to come to a proper sense of the dreadful situation in which you have placed yourself. Of that short time, I hope that you will make full use, and that you will come into the presence of your Redeemer so fortified with a sincere repentance as to give you a hope in His mercy—a mercy that cannot be extended to you in this world.'

The Judge paused for a moment, and continued :

'Prisoner at the Bar, have you anything to say why sentence should not be passed on you, according to Law?'

To this the prisoner answered, 'No,' and the Judge proceeded to pass sentence :

'Stephen Sullivan, you shall be removed from the place where you stand to the goal, and on Thursday next, 27th July, 1820, you shall be removed from there to the common place of execution, where you shall be hanged by the neck until you are dead, and your body given to the County Hospital for dissection—and may the Lord have mercy on your soul!'

During the trial, the prisoner's countenance underwent

no change—until towards the close, when he seemed to feel that all was over with him.

❧ 13 Expiation

> Unrespited, unpitied, unreprieved.
> JOHN MILTON

ON THE FOLLOWING THURSDAY, at four o'clock in the afternoon—barely forty-eight hours after his conviction, Stephen Sullivan was taken from the old city gaol to Gallows Green, in Singland (a suburb of Limerick), for execution.

The crowds assembled on this occasion were far larger than usually attended those barbarous spectacles, partly owing to the great interest excited by the commission of so appalling a murder, and partly owing to a rumour which had spread through the city, that Sullivan had made a confession of the tragic deed, in which he, himself, was the principal actor, and the only person living who could throw any light on it.

His countenance had undergone much alteration in the brief period since his trial. It was marked with guilt and care, penitence and sorrow.

When he arrived at the place of execution, he continued a long time in prayer with the clergyman who attended him, and was at one period so weak that it became necessary to fetch him a drink of water. He then ascended the platform with a fairly firm step, and, having expressed a wish to make a statement as to his part in the crime, several well-known gentlemen encircled the gallows, when the attendant clergyman addressed him as follows :

Now, Sullivan, remember that you are going before the Almighty God! and recollect that the damnation of your soul will be the consequence, if you tell a lie as to the murder of Ellen Hanley—more particularly, as it involves the character of another.

You can have no interest but to tell the truth; so, *in the name of God! as you hope for your salvation, tell what you know.*

Sullivan then made the following statement :

71

'I declare before the Almighty that *I am guilty of the murder!* but it was Mr. Scanlan who put me up to it. We were walking on the strand when he said to me that he should get rid of the girl. He was at me then for some days before I consented—which I unfortunately did. He then bought a boat from one Pat Case, for the express purpose of destroying her, and got an iron chain and ring made by a smith in Kilrush, to tie around her neck. Ellen Walsh, Mitchell, and other persons came with us in the boat from Kilrush to Carrig-island, where we stopped the night.

'Mr. Scanlan and I went to Ballylongford, where we bought some spirits, and that day it was intended to murder her, between Carrig-island and Moneypoint. Mr. Scanlan went out of the boat, in order that when he was absent I should have it done; *but when I looked on her innocent face, my heart shuddered, and I did not know how I could do it.*

'When Mr. Scanlan returned, he gave me many sour looks, and was mad with me because I did not murder her. I then went out of the boat and bought two shillings' worth of bread, a pound of butter, and about three half-pints of whiskey, and we stayed out that night until next morning. We then continued that day together. When Mr. Scanlan got up to go out of the boat, Mrs. Scanlan asked him where he was going. He answered that he was going to Glin by a short-cut, to prepare lodging for her, where she would stay that night. He then made me take some spirits, and desired that I should get more from her, if necessary.

'Scanlan settled the rope, and spliced a loop to it, which he put round a large stone, in order that I should lose no time, and left everything ready for me in the boat. *In the course of that night I murdered her,* and the following day I went to Glin, where I saw Mr. Scanlan, who asked me, "Did I do that?" I told him I did. "All is right," said he.'

The unfortunate criminal was then asked if he knew what was the reason that Scanlan left the boat. He said it was so that he should be seen in Glin, if the murder was found out.

He was also asked what was Scanlan's motive for having her murdered, to which he replied that he did not know, unless it was that she always called him her husband. To another question, he said that he had never robbed her, but he certainly took the ring spoken of.

After some pause, the unfortunate man said that it was the neglect of his religion which had led him to the commission of this act; for, had he taken good advice, he would not meet this unhappy end, and he hoped his example, to all who saw and heard him, would be a warning.

He continued to pray most fervently, hoping that the Great God would forgive him his sins, and, as the cart moved off, his last words were:

'The Lord have mercy on me!'

The rumour that Sullivan would make a full confession, which was rife in the City of Limerick on the morning of the execution, was founded on something more than mere speculation.

After his conviction on Tuesday, he made a full and free admission of his guilt in the gaol, in the presence of several people, and described the mode of the Colleen Bawn's destruction.

When the boat was about in the middle of the Shannon, he stood up and took a musket in his hand, with which he made a blow at her head; but it missed her head and he struck her arm, which was broken. He then beat her with the gun until she was dead, after which he trussed her up, and, with the large stone attached to the rope, flung the body into the river, where it sank immediately.

Thus ended the final chapter in the tragic story of the Colleen Bawn, a story of infinite pathos and stark, unrelieved tragedy.

She sleeps in the little country churchyard of Burrane, not far from where her body was washed ashore, and about five hundred yards from the river which knew her very brief happiness.

Gerald Griffin
The Collegians
adapted by
Sigerson Clifford

ANVIL BOOKS LIMITED

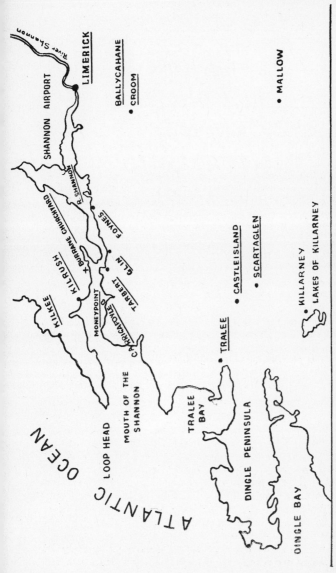

Places mentioned in the Colleen Bawn story are underlined on this map of the district which is based on the Ordnance Survey by permission of the Minister for Finance.

❧ 1 Eily Leaves Home

IT WAS LATE AND DARK on the night of March the sixteenth when Mihil O'Connor, the ropemaker, and his beautiful daughter, Eily, left the Owen's house in Garryowen, where they had been entertained, for their home in Limerick. Mihil walked along smartly, anxious to get home as quickly as possible. Owen's hospitality had been so generous that he had forgotten, until his host reminded him, that this was the night the youthful inhabitants of Limerick celebrated the arrival of Saint Patrick's Day in the morning by promenading the streets, playing national airs and shouting like Red Indians whenever the band stopped to draw its breath.

'Some of the lads in the procession,' Owen said, 'might be playin' their thricks upon Miss Eily.'

Mihil and Eily had completed over half their journey and were turning from a narrow lane at the head of Mungret Street when they found their way barred by the noisy laughing mob of revellers moving towards them. They slipped into a doorway and quietly waited for the procession to pass by, but they did not escape unnoticed. Some of the bloods carried lanterns, and the beautiful Eily felt her cheeks tingle at their comments. One fellow who didn't believe in wasting any time made as if to kiss her. It was too much for old Mihil. He lifted his stick and stretched the scoundrel with a blow on the temple. Immediately a dozen weapons were raised to cut the old man to the ground, but before they fell two young men in the dress of boatmen slipped between the O'Connors and the attackers and persuaded the latter to withdraw. Not satisfied with having rescued them, the taller of the two conducted them to their door, saying little on the way, and taking his leave as soon as they were safe.

'That's a right gallant young gentleman whoever he is,' Old Mihil remarked, as Hardress Cregan vanished into the darkness in search of his servant, the hunchback, Danny Mann.

Eily said nothing. She had met Hardress at the open-air dance in Garryowen and was already in love with him, and the future looked bleak enough. The Cregans resided in Killarney, where they owned some property, and they were accepted by the gentry as equals. Mr. Cregan rode to hounds, and his imperious wife was a stepsister to Mrs. Chute of Castle Chute, thus related to one of the most influential families in County Limerick. Their son, Hardress, with Danny Mann as helper, spent most of his time sailing his pleasure-boat, *Nora Creina,* along the River Shannon, and the pair were as well-known in Limerick as in their native Killarney. Eily, who knew the class-conscious Ireland of the day, could not see the snobbish Mrs. Cregan accepting a ropemaker's daughter as an equal, whatever Hardress might say. She guessed, quite rightly, that the fox-hunting crowd would prefer to keep her in the kitchen where, they considered, she would be more at home than in the drawing-room.

It was something Hardress Cregan saw more clearly than Eily, but he wanted her and soon he married her secretly. Not even her father knew about it. The more Eily thought about it afterwards the less it seemed like a proper marriage at all.

'Do you remember the morning of our marriage?' Eily asked Hardress when they were on their way to Killarney, after she had stolen away from her father's home. 'I can never put that frightful morning out of my mind. 'Tis always before my eyes. The little room inside the sacristy, and the candles burning on the small table, and the grey dawn just breaking through the window. We did not marry as other people do, in their families or in the open daylight. We married in secret like criminals in prison, without preparation, without confession, or communion, or repentance. We chose a priest that was disgraced by his bishop, to give us that great sacrament for money. Afterwards, I was just going to lift the latch of my father's door when I found I had forgotten the priest's certificate. I went back to the chapel as fast as I could walk. The certificate was there upon the table, the candles were burning, and the clergyman was sitting upright in his chair— a dead man!'

One month after the secret marriage Eily Cregan was still in her father's house. Myles na Gopaleen Murphy, a goodnatured farmer from Killarney, who travelled through the country selling Kerry ponies, called to ask old Mihil's permission to marry his daughter. The old ropemaker was delighted with the proposal, for Myles, as well as being a fine figure of a man, was a snug fellow with a very comfortable property, and he pressed his daughter to accept Myles or give a good reason for her refusal. Eily's reply was to throw her blue cloak over her shoulders and walk out the door.

Old Mihil never saw her alive again.

Eily's flight from home put her husband in a quandary. Afraid of his mother's censure and the ridicule of his friends, he still kept the story of his marriage secret. He solved the problem by finding her lodgings in a lonely cottage among the mountains of Killarney. The cottage belonged to Phil Naughten and his wife, Poll, sister to Danny Mann.

2 Kerry Honeymoon

WHEN HARDRESS RODE FROM KILLARNEY into the mountains where he had hidden his wife he found Eily anxiously awaiting his coming. To a girl used to the whirl and excitement of Limerick city the quietness of her rocky refuge was appalling. For company she had the eagle screaming above the crags, the fox barking among the furze, the wild goats complaining as they jumped from rock to rock. Then, to add to her troubles, Poll Naughten terrified her.

For feats of daring, Queen Maeve of Connaught was only a ballet-dancer compared with Mrs. Phil Naughten. She was known throughout Munster as Fighting Poll of the Reeks, a name she earned the hard way by dashing into the thick of the faction-fights swinging a stocking with a stone in the toe of it, if there was no spare shillelagh handy. She drank whiskey enough to float Noah's Ark, she cursed and swore like a brigade of troopers, and she had a tongue that could make words stand on their tippy-toes and spit in your eye. Judging by her face and hair some sailor from the Spanish Armada had climbed thankfully out of the cold sea to find refuge among the branches of her family tree. She was over six feet tall and built like an Amazon.

When Hardress was embracing his wife at the open door a piercing shout from above distrubed him. He looked up and saw Poll standing on the turf, watching him keenly with angry bloodshot eyes.

'Ha, ha, my children, my two fine clever children, is it there ye are!' she roared. 'Oh, the luck of me, that it wasn't a lad like you I married; a clever boy with the red blood running under his yellow skin, instead of the mane withered disciple that calls my house his own this day. I might have been a lady if I liked. Oh, the luck of me! Five tall young men, every one of them a patthern for a faction, and all, all dead in their graves, down, down, and no one left but that picture of misery, that calls himself my husband.'

She jumped down and stood in front of them.

'If it wasn't for the whiskey,' she added, 'my heart would break with the thoughts of it. Five tall young men, brothers every one, and they to die, and he to live! Wouldn't it kill the Danes to think of it! Give me the price of the whiskey.'

'You have had enough already, Poll,' Hardress told her.

'I only had two drams and that isn't half enough,' Poll shouted.

She turned to Eily.

'Coax him, my heart, my child, to give me the price of the whiskey.'

'Your young mistress does not wish to see you any more drunk than you are,' Hardress told the Amazon.

Poll whirled on him in a fury.

'*My* mistress! The ropemaker's daughter! The poor silly craythur. Is it because I call you my masther that I'd call her a lady and my misthress? Give me the price of the whiskey or I'll tear the crooked eyes out o' your yellow face! Give me it or I'll give my misthress more kicks than ha'pence the next time I catch her alone in the house, and you away coorting an' divarting at Killarney.'

'Cool yourself, Poll,' Hardress warned, 'or I'll make you cool.'

It was the wrong tactic to quieten Fighting Poll when her temper was up.

'You a gentleman!' she shouted for all the hills to hear. 'There isn't a noggin of genteel blood in the veins of your whole seed, breed and generation. You stingy, bone-polishing, tawny-faced, beggarly, mane-spirited mohawk. And signs on, see what a misthress you brought over us! While others looked up you looked down. I often seen a worm turning to a butterfly but I never heard of a butter-fly turning to a worm in my life, before. I'll lay a noggin, if the dochtors open you when ye die, they won't find such a thing as a heart in your whole yellow carcase, only a cowld gizzard like the turkey's.'

Hardress saw Eily's pretty face growing pale with fear, and he realised that Fighting Poll had won another battle. He tossed her half-a-crown and watched her hurry down the road to the shebeen for whiskey.

Before he left that evening Hardress told Eily that the time was not yet ripe to tell his mother of their secret marriage. She heard this with pain and grief, but without remonstrance. She cried like a child at parting with him; and, after he had ridden away, remained leaning against the jamb of the door with her moistened handkerchief placed against her cheek in an attitude of musing sorrow. The marriage-bed she had made was much harder than she expected, and she had to lie in it alone.

※ 3 Hardress Regrets

Unaware that she already had a daughter-in-law, Mrs. Cregan, mother of Hardress, had invited Anne Chute to come from her Limerick castle to keep her company in Killarney. Mrs. Cregan thought it time that her roving son, who seemed to spend most of his time boating on the Shannon with his hunchback servant, Danny Mann, found himself a wife and settled down in holy and happy matri-mony. In Mrs. Cregan's eyes Anne Chute was the perfect choice for Hardress. She was beautiful, sensible, musical and one of his own genteel class. She was also madly in love with Hardress, who had never given her a second look. Indeed, he thought her cold and distant, and spoiled by too much high education.

A few days after his noisy meeting with Fighting Poll of the Reeks, Hardress was at home, gazing idly through the window, while Mrs. Cregan was arranging china on a table in the middle of the room.

'Mother, is Anne Chute not feeling too well?' Hardress asked. 'She's walking around like a ghost with nothing to say to anyone.'

'Anne has met with the usual fate of young ladies at her age,' Mrs. Cregan told him. 'She is deep in love. In fact, I never saw a girl so much in love in my life.'

'Who is the happy fellow, Mother? Captain Gibson?'

'Try another guess,' Mrs. Cregan said.

'Kyrle Daly, then?'

'Not Kyrle Daly, either,' his mother told him. 'The truth is, Hardress, she loves you.'

Hardress flushed with pleasure at the news. Conquests were not strangers to him but this was a big one and he had not even lifted his little finger to achieve it.

'How on earth do you know, Mother?' he asked with a smile.

'The dear child confided in me,' Mrs. Cregan told him. 'And, what is more, I told Anne that you were as deeply in love with her as she with you.'

'But I am not in love with her,' Hardress said, alarmed at the turn events were taking.

'And why not?' Mrs. Cregan asked, severely.

'Because I have pledged myself to another,' Hardress told her.

Mrs. Cregan stared at him as if stunned.

'And who is this person?' she asked. 'Is she superior to Anne Chute in rank and fortune?'

'Far otherwise, Mother.'

'In talent then, or manner?'

'Still far beneath Anne,' Hardress admitted.

Mrs. Cregan snorted with disgust.

'I take it this person is poor, low-born, silly and vulgar, and yet you have pledged yourself to marry her,' she said with a forced smile.

'I am afraid there is no escaping it now, Mother,' Hardress told her.

'Break off this vulgar engagement,' Mrs. Cregan threatened, 'or you shall never possess a guinea of your inheritance. Come, sir, make your choice.'

'It is already made,' Hardress said with a mournful dignity as he moved towards the door.

It would have put an end to all discussion on the subject if Hardress had informed his mother that he was already married. He was aware of this and yet he could not tell her that it was so. It was a decision both mother and son would have ample reason to regret.

The revelation that the very beautiful and very desirable Anne Chute was in love with him made Hardress worry more than ever over his hasty marriage with Eily. The gilt had rubbed off the romantic gingerbread even before this, and Hardress had many bad moments dreaming of the hour when he must introduce Eily to his rich and fashionable friends. He pictured the bashfulness, the awkwardness, and the homeliness of speech and accent with which the ropemaker's daughter received their compliments, and he shuddered. He had a particularly bad moment one night in his sleep when he saw Eily at the crowded dining-table, peeling a potato with her fingernails.

During the few weeks that followed the conversation with his mother, Eily perceived a rapid and fearful change in the temper and appearance of her husband. His visits were shorter, his eye troubled, his voice deep and broken, and he no longer conversed with that noisy frankness and gaiety which was his custom when he was at peace with the world. To Eily he spoke sometimes with coldness and impatience. Fighting Poll and her husband, Phil, found him altogether reserved and haughty, not that Poll lost much sleep over his attitude to her, as long as he didn't neglect to give her, to use her own expression, 'The price of a pound of candles' now and again. Even Danny Mann, who was nearer to him than most people, found himself snarled at when he tried to tempt Hardress into a conversation. One night Hardress arrived at the cottage much the worse for brandy, and Eily experienced for the first time, and with an aching heart, one of the keenest anxieties of married life.

'Hardress,' she said to him in the morning when he was preparing to depart, after one of his gloomy silences, "I won't let you go among those fine ladies any more, if you be thinking of them always when you come to see me again.'

'What do you mean?' Hardress asked sharply.

'Those fine ladies that don't know you're married to

Eily O'Connor, I'm talking about. I was wedded, sir, a couple of months ago, to one Mr. Hardress Cregan, a very nice gentleman that I'm very fond of.'

'Too fond, perhaps,' Hardress said, gruffly.

'I'm afraid so, rightly speaking, although I hope *he* doesn't think so. But he told me when he brought me down to Killarney that he was going to speak to his friends and to ask for their forgiveness for himself and Eily. And there's nearly two months now since I came and what I have to charge myself with is that I am too fond of my husband, and that I don't like to vex him by speaking about it, as may be it would be my duty to do. And, besides, I don't keep my husband in proper order at all. I let him stop out sometimes for many days together, and then I'm very angry with him, but when he comes I'm so foolish and so glad to see him that I can't look cross or speak a hard word, if I was to get all Ireland for it. And more than that again, I'm not at all sure how he spends his time when he is away, and I don't ever question him properly about it. And, besides all this, I think my husband has something weighing upon his mind, and I don't make him tell it to me, as a good wife ought to do. Do you think any of the fine ladies has taken his fancy? Or do you think he's growing tired of Eily? Or that he doesn't think so much of her now that he knows her better?'

'Well, then,' Hardress said, rising and addressing her sternly, 'my advice to you is this. As long as you live never presume to inquire into your husband's secrets. That's right, laugh at me. You have the best right to laugh, for you are the gainer. Curse on your beauty—curse on my own folly— for I have been undone by both. I am sick of you! You have disgusted me! I will ease my heart by telling you the whole. If I seek the society of other women it is because I do not find among them your meanness and vulgarity. I get drunk and make myself the beast you think I am, to forget the iron chain that binds me to you.'

Terrified with the turn things had taken, Eily knelt before him and flung her arms about his legs to keep him from going.

'Oh, Hardress, my husband, stay with me! Think how far I am from home. Remember all you promised me and how I believed you. Do not leave me alone in this terrible place,' she begged through her tears.

As he struggled to free himself from her arms she fainted.

When she came to her senses Hardress was gone and the worried face of Fighting Poll was bent over her.

'Ah, there she draws the breath,' Poll said with relief. 'Oh, wirra, missis, what brought you out on your face and hands on the middle of the floor, that way?'

Remembering all that had gone before, Eily lay back on the floor and wept.

As Hardress, hurrying from the cottage, passed the lonely little bridge which crosses the stream above the dark lake he heard a familiar voice calling him from the clouds. Looking over his shoulder to the summit of the Purple Mountain, he saw Danny Mann nearly a thousand feet above him driving a small herd of goats belonging to Phil Naughten, his brother-in-law. Hardress turned off the road and began to climb the mountain towards him.

'It's well for you, Master Hardress,' Danny greeted him. 'that hasn't a flock of goats to be hunting after this morning. My heart is broke from them, that's what it is. What a fine day this would be for the water. You don't ever care to take a sail now, sir?'

Hardress made him no reply but stared at the mountain with brooding eyes, while Danny watched him keenly.

'There's something troubling you, Master Hardress,' Danny said. 'And 'tisn't now nor to-day nor yesterday, I seen it either. If there's anything Danny Mann can do to serve you, only say the word.'

Hardress looked at him a few moments in silence.

'I *am* troubled,' he told him. 'I was a fool, Danny, when I refused to listen to your advice on one occasion.

Danny remembered the occasion immediately.

'That was the time I told you not to go agin your station, and to have no call to Eily O'Connor.'

'It was,' Hardress admitted.

'I thought it would be this way,' Danny said. 'I thought, all along, that Eily was no wife for you, Master Hardress. It was not in nature she could be. A poor man's daughter, without money, or manners, or book-learning, or one haporth. I told you that, Master Hardress, but you wouldn't hear me, and this is the way of it now.'

'I was to blame, Danny, and I am suffering for it,' Hardress told him. 'What am I to do now?'

Danny had the solution in a moment.

'Sorra trouble would I ever give myself about her only send her home packing to her father, and give her no thanks.'

'And what would my friends say when the story is noised throughout Kerry and Limerick?' Hardress said bitterly. 'I should be despised for ever.'

'I never thought of that,' Danny admitted, nodding his head. 'That's a horse of another colour. Why, then, I'll tell what I'd do. Pay her passage out to Quebec, and put her aboard a three-master without ever saying a word to anyone. Do by her as you'd do by that glove you have on your hand. Make it come off as it come on, and if it fits too tight, take the knife to it.'

'What do you mean?' Hardress asked.

'Only give me the word and Eily O'Connor will never trouble you any more,' Danny told him. 'Don't ask me any questions at all only, if you're agreeable, take off that glove and give it to me for a token. That'll be enough. Leave the rest to Danny.'

Hardress stared at his servant in horror as the exact meaning of Danny Mann's intentions became clear to him. He shot out his hands and, squeezing his fingers around Danny's throat, shook him until the fellow was purple in the face.

'You damn scoundrel!' Hardress cried. 'If you ever harm a hair of Eily's head, I will tear your vile body limb from limb!'

Then, flinging the half-choked Danny Mann on the heather, he turned on his heel and hurried down the mountain as if the devil was running at his elbow.

4 Uncle Edward

TOWARDS NIGHT-FALL Eily was lying back in her bed bewildered by the events of the morning, when she heard somebody approaching the cottage, singing a come-all-ye in a low voice as he came. She sat up as she recognised the voice. It belonged to Lowry Looby, a carman employed by Mr. Daly, a middleman who owned a successful business in Limerick. Lowry had been one of the many suitors for Eily's affections, and as she listened it occurred to her that her father had found out her hiding-place and sent

Lowry to take her home. In fact, Lowry was returning to Limerick after a journey to the Cork Buttermarket, and decided to drop in on Fighting Poll for a night's lodgings, unaware that Mihil O'Connor's beautiful daughter was an unhappy guest under the same piece of thatch.

As Eily listened to Lowry talking to the Naughtens in the kitchen she saw that Lowry's visit had been a chance one, and her secret was still safe from him. She decided to write to her father by Lowry, to make him aware of her safety, and of her hope to meet him again in honour if not in happiness. While she arranged her writing materials at a small table the door opened and Poll entered.

'Poll, do you know who that man in the kitchen is?' Eily asked.

'That's Lowry Looby, a scoundrel from Limerick,' Poll said.

'I want to caution you against saying anything about me while he's here,' Eily told her. 'Mr. Hardress wouldn't like it.'

'Devil a bit the wiser of it I'll leave him,' Poll promised.

'I also want him to deliver a letter in Limerick for me,' Eily said. 'But don't tell him who gave it to you, no matter how many questions he asks.'

When Lowry got the letter which was addressed to *Mr. Dunat O'Leary, Haircutter, Garryowen,* he wondered who the hidden stranger was that thought Foxy Dunat, the hair-butcher, worthy of correspondence. The contents were brief. Dunat was to call on his neighbour, Mihil O'Connor, and tell him that his daughter was safe and in good health. Had Eily put her father's name and address on the letter the mystery of the stranger in the inner room would be solved immediately by Lowry, who could put two and two together as good as any scholar. He made many enquiries as to the name and quality of the shy lodger, all of which Poll ignored, and he left for Limerick in the morning, telling himself that 'It flogged the world for queerness.'

The first weeks of winter swept rapidly away, and Eily neither saw nor heard from Hardress. Her situation with the Naughtens was becoming more unpleasant, now she seemed to be out of favour with her patron. She had maintained her place on the sunny side of Poll's esteem by slipping the virago small sums of money from time to time, although her conscience told her that these donations were bound to find a resting-place in the till of the shebeen owner down the glen. But now her stock of money was running low, and there was no sign of her husband appearing to replenish her purse.

She sat down and wrote him a short pathetic letter.

My dear Hardress,
Do not leave me here to spend the whole winter alone. If Eily has done anything to offend you, come and tell her so, but remember she is now away from every friend in the whole world. Even if you are still in the same mind as when you left me, come at all events for once and let me go back to my father. If you wish it, nobody besides us three shall ever know what you were to your own
Eily.

She gave the letter to Danny Mann to deliver, but there came no answer from her husband.

The wintry year rolled on in barreriness and gloom, casting an air of iron majesty and grandeur over the savage scenery in which she dwelt, and bringing close to her threshold the first Christmas which she had ever spent away from home. Christmas Eve found her still anxiously looking forward to the return of her husband. The morning had brought with it a black frost, and Eily sat down to a comfortless breakfast. No longer waited on by the Naughtens, she was now obliged to procure and arrange all the materials for her meals herself. The sugarbowl was empty, and she looked into the kitchen where Poll was hunched beside the fire.

'I have no sugar, Poll,' Eily said.

Poll glowered at her.

'Well, what hurt? Can't you put a double allowance of cream in the tay, and drink it raw for once?'

'But this is a fast day and cream is forbidden,' Eily told her.

'Ah, choke it for work!' Poll said. 'I haven't a spoonful of groceries in the house, girl. Give me the money by-an'-by, when I'm going into town for the Christmas candle, and I'll buy plenty sugar for you.'

'But I have no money, Poll.'

'No money, is it? And isn't it upon yourself we're depending to get in the things for Christmas Day!' Poll protested.

'Well, I haven't a farthing,' Eily admitted.

Poll stared hard at her in horror.

'Didn't you tell me yourself the other day that you had half a crown in hiding for me?'

'I gave it to Danny,' Eily told her. 'I was expecting some money but it hasn't come.'

It was too much for Poll's limited patience. She burst in the room-door with a mighty fist and towered above her frightened lodger, her face distorted with rage.

'And that is my thanks?' she screamed. 'Cocking you up with bread and tay this morning, and not a brown penny in your pocket to compensate me! Go look after Danny now if you want your breakfast!'

And, seizing two corners of the tablecloth, she lifted it and flung the breakfast things into the fireplace.

Speechless with terror Eily watched, and then the forlorn helplessness of her position possessed her mind, and she fell back into her seat in a violent fit of hysterics.

It brought Poll to heel quicker than a cudgel. She ran to Eily and put her arms about her like a mother.

'Whisht now, a graw geal,' she comforted her. 'What ails you at all? Sure you know 'twas only funning I was. Tell me anything now in the world you want done and I'll do it for you, my little childeen.'

The promise helped Eily to recover quickly enough.

'Poll, there is one thing that you can do for me, and it will help me greatly,' she told her.

'And what thing is that, my heart?'

'Lend me one of the ponies and get me a boy that can show me the way to Castle Island,' Eily said.

'And what business would carry you to Castle Island?' Poll asked.

'My uncle lives there,' Eily said. 'I'm sure he will give me some money.'

The thought of Eily returning from Castle Island with a bulging purse of money had Poll on her toes immediately. Within half an hour the saddled pony was standing outside the cottage door and, after promising Poll that she would be back on the following day, Eily set off on her journey to her Uncle Edward, the parish priest of Castle Island.

When Father Edward O'Connor was a curate in Limerick Eily was accustomed to spend a lot of her time in his company, but he was appointed to his mountainy parish far from the busy city streets and she saw him no more. It was a promotion Father Edward regretted. In Limerick he had comfortable lodgings, a civil landlady, regular hours of discipline and the society of his oldest friends, and Eily to amuse him with her lighthearted chatter as she took charge of the tea table. In Castle Island he had a small cold house on the side of a mountain, total seclusion from the company of his equals, and a fearful increase of responsibility.

He was in his small parlour on Christmas Day, enjoying a late and frugal breakfast, when the parish clerk opened the door.

'A girl, Father Edward, that's abroad, and would want to see you, if you please.'

'Do you know who she is, Jim?' Father Edward asked.

'No, Father, in regard she keeps her head down, and her handkerchief to her mouth. I stooped to have a peep underneath, but if I stooped low she stooped lower, and left me just as wise as I was in the beginning.'

'Send her in,' Father Edward ordered. 'I don't like this secrecy.'

Father Edward's eyes flickered over his mysterious visitor as she entered. She was young and well formed, and clothed in a blue cloak and bonnet which concealed her face effectively.

'Well, my good girl, what is your business with me?' he asked.

To his astonishment she knelt down suddenly at his feet, uncovered her face, and began to weep.

'Oh, Uncle Edward, don't you know me?' she cried.

Father Edward stared at her silently for some moments. Then after placing her in a chair he resumed his own seat, and covered his face with his hand, while Eily continued to weep loudly.

'Come, come, don't cry,' Father O'Connor told her. 'Ah, little Eily, I never thought we would meet like this.'

'Please forgive me, Uncle,' Eily sobbed. 'I did it for the best, indeed.'

'Did it for the best!' Father Edward said sternly. 'I won't speak of my own sufferings since I heard of your disappearance. But there is your old father who has not had one moment's peace of mind since you left him. He was here with me a week since, and I was never more shocked in all my life, such was his appearance. You cry, but you would cry more bitterly if you saw him. Was that done for the best, Eily?'

'Uncle,' Eily told him through her tears, 'I am guilty of disobedience only. I was married a month before I left my father.'

Father Edward was delighted to find his niece was not the abandoned woman he thought she was.

'Well, well, Eily, that's splendid news,' he told her. 'The general supposition was something different. I am very glad of this, my child. It will be a great comfort to your father. But where do you stay now, and who is your husband?'

'I am not at liberty to tell you, Uncle,' Eily said. 'My husband does not know of my coming here, and I dare not think of telling what he commanded that I should keep secret.'

'More secrecy,' Father Edward sighed, rising from his seat and pacing the room. 'I say again I do not like this affair. What reasons has your husband for this extra-ordinary concealment?'

'I cannot tell you his reasons just now,' Eily said timidly. Her uncle was more than a little annoyed.

'Where do you hear Mass on Sundays, or do you hear it regularly at all?' he asked.

Eily's drooping head and long silence let him know the answer.

'Did you hear Mass a single Sunday since you left home?' he asked with increasing amazement.

'Not one, Uncle,' Eily whispered.

'God forgive you, child,' he said. 'Why then did you come to see me if you have no power to tell me all the information I require so that I can help you?'

'I came so that you may tell my father all that I have told you,' Eily said. 'Tell him also that I hope it will not be long until I ask his pardon for all the sorrow I have caused him. I will return now to my husband and persuade him, if I can, to come here to Castle Island with me again this week.'

The more Father Edward thought on Eily's strange husband the less he liked him.

'You are married, Eily, I think, to someone who is not

very proud of his wife,' he told her. 'He does not appear a person fit to be trusted or obeyed. It seems to me this man is a tyrant. Why don't you remain here with me and write him a letter telling where you may be found? I should like to have a few words with him.'

'I cannot stay, Uncle,' Eily said. 'I love my husband far too much to stay away from him. I must go now as I promised I would return this evening.'

Father Edward pressed some silver into her hand as she was leaving.

'It is a long time since I gave you a Christmas box,' he said with a smile. 'Goodbye, my child. I hope this will be the last time I shall have to part from you without being able to tell your name.'

Eily left the house with tears in her eyes, and turned her pony towards the Reeks where Fighting Poll Naughten was waiting for 'the price of a pound of candles' to tide her over the Christmas.

5 Eily's Last Journey

EILY WASTED NO TIME on her journey homewards, and it was nearly dusk when the pony turned in upon the little craggy road which runs upwards through the Gap. The evening was calm and frosty, and every footfall of the animal was echoed from the opposite cliffs like the stroke of a hammer. Chilled by the nipping air, and afraid of attracting the attention of any occasional straggler, Eily had drawn her blue cloak around her face and was proceeding swiftly in the direction of Naughten's cottage when she heard voices on the far side of a hedge she was passing.

'Seven pound ten and a pint of whiskey, the same as I had for the dead match of her from Father O'Connor, the priest, eastwards in Castle Island! Say the word now. Seven pound ten, or lave it there.'

'Seven pound,' the second voice said with finality.

'Well, then, being relations as we are, I won't break your word, although the pony is worth twice it,' the first voice agreed to the bargain.

In her first start of surprise at hearing this well-remembered voice, Eily had dropped the mantle from her face.

Before she could replace it a man sprang up on the hedge and stood there staring at her.

'Eily!' he said, 'Eily O'Connor, is it you I see at last?'

Eily, with lowered eyes, replied in a whisper that was barely audible.

' 'Tis, Myles.'

Myles na Gopaleen, her first declared admirer and the cause of her present exile from her father's house, approached and stood beside her, his eyes big with surprise.

'I saw your father last week,' he told her. 'He's still at his old work on the rope-walk.'

'Did you speak to him, Myles?' Eily asked.

'I was afraid to go near him,' Myles confessed. ' 'Tis me he blames on account of you running away from home, the time we were tormenting you to marry me.'

'There is only one person to blame and that is myself,' Eily told him.

Myles refused to believe it.

'Are you going far a-past the Gap? Let me guide the pony for you,' he offered.

'No, Myles,' Eily refused gently. 'Where I am going, I must go alone.'

'Alone?' Myles echoed. 'Sure, 'tisn't to part from me you will now?'

'I must, indeed, Myles,' Eily said.

'And what will I say to your father when I go and tell him that I saw Eily and spoke to her, and that I know no more?' Myles asked.

'Tell him that I am sorry for the trouble I gave him, and that before many days I hope to ask his pardon on my knees,' Eily told him.

'And amn't I to know where you stop itself?' Myles asked.

Eily shook her head.

'Not now, Myles. If you knew where I am staying it would do me a great injury. Goodnight, Myles.'

'Say no more, achree,' Myles told her. 'The word is enough. Cover up your hands in your cloak, and hide your face from the frost. I don't like to see you going up this lonesome glen alone, and a winter night coming on, and not knowing where you're steering, or who you're trusting to. Eily, be said by me and let me go with you.'

Eily again refused and gave her hand to Myles, who

pressed it between his, and seemed as slow to part with it as if it was a purse of gold. When she was gone from him Myles remained gazing after her until she disappeared among the shadows of the rocks.

It was the eve of Little Christmas before Eily received an answer to the letter she had sent to her husband.

She was sitting by the fire, listening anxiously to every sound that approached the door. Poll Naughten was arranging at a small table the three-branched candle with which the vigil of Little Christmas was celebrated. A shadow fell upon the threshold and Eily started from her chair. It was Danny Mann. She looked for a second figure but it did not appear, and she returned to her chair with a look of agony and disappointment.

'Where's your master? Isn't he coming?' Poll asked, while she touched a lighted rush to one of the candles.

'He isn't,' Danny replied. 'He has something else to do.'

He approached Eily who noticed, as he handed her the note, that he looked more pale than usual, and that his eyes quivered with an uncertain and gloomy fire. She read it and then, letting her hand fall lifeless by her side, she leaned back against the wall feeling cold and deserted. Danny avoided looking at her in this condition and stooped forward with his hands expanded over the fire. Unaware of what had taken place, Poll devoted her attentions to the candles. Again Eily read the unkind loveless words that dismissed her from her husband's life.

I *am* still in the same mind as when I left you. I accept your proposal. Put yourself under the bearer's care, and he will restore you to your father.

While Eily stood there reading and remembering the warmth and tenderness of Hardress in the early days of their marriage, she heard Danny's whisper in her ear.

'If you're agreeable to do what's in that paper, Miss Eily, I have a boy below at the Gap with a horse and car, and you can set off tonight if you like.'

Eily nodded sadly and went into the little room which, during the honeymoon, had been furnished and decorated for her own use. With hurried and trembling hands she got herself ready for the departure. She dropped her clothes into a trunk, and for once she tied on her bonnet and cloak without consulting the mirror. Everything was all over now. It was a happy dream but it was ended. In a few minutes she was back in the kitchen, dressed for the journey.

'Danny, I am ready,' she said, in a faint, small voice.

'Ready?' cried Poll. 'Is it going you are, achree?'

'Goodbye to you, Poll,' Eily said, in the same small voice. 'I am sorry I have only thanks to give at parting, but I will not forget you when it is in my power. I left my things in the room. I will send for them some other time.'

'And where is it you're going?' Poll demanded. 'Danny, what's all this about?'

'What business is it of your's anyway?' Danny replied. 'Or of mine either? It's the master's bidding, and you can ask him why he done it when he comes, if you want to know.'

'But the night will rain,' Poll protested. 'It will be a bad night. I seen the clouds gathering for thunder and I coming down the mountain.'

'I must go tonight, Poll,' Eily told her.

'If it be the master's bidding, it must be right, no doubt,' Poll decided, looking in wonder at Eily's dejected face. 'But it's a quare story, that's what it is. Won't you ate anything itself?'

'No, Poll,' Eily refused the offer. 'Maybe, Danny might like something before we go.'

'I'll drink a drop if you have it,' Danny said.

Poll handed him a bottle from the dresser and he drank the contents at a draught. Then, handing back the empty bottle to his sister, he followed Eily into the night.

✦ 6 Hardress Hears News

EILY HAD not been gone very long from the cottage when the thunder-storm predicted by Fighting Poll broke upon the mountains. The rain poured in torrents, and the thunder clattered among the crags and precipices with a thousand short reverberations. Phil Naughten, who had entered soon after the storm began, was seated with his wife at their small supper table, Poll complaining heavily of the assault made by Danny on her spirit flask, which she now discovered to be empty.

Suddenly the latch of the door was raised and Hardress Cregan entered, with confusion and terror in his appearance. The dark frieze great-coat which covered him was drenched with rain, and his face was flushed and glistening with the beating of the weather. He closed the door with difficulty against the strong wind and stood there, keeping his left hand on the latch.

'I am afraid I have come too late,' he said. 'Is Danny here?'

'No, sir,' Phil told him. 'He's gone these two hours.'

'And Eily?'

'Eily went along with him,' Phil said. 'He gave her papers that made her go.'

Hardress leaned his back against the door, exhausted after his long journey on foot in the height of the storm. He had hurried to save Eily from her fate and he was too late. He stood there, his eyes on the ground, pondering his situation. He had promised his mother that he would marry Anne Chute, and Anne had consented to become his wife. It was necessary to remove Eily from the scene, and Danny Mann was the fellow to do the deed.

'Danny,' he had asked his servant, some days before, 'do you remember a conversation which I had with you some weeks since, on the Purple Mountain?'

Danny had remembered it well.

'You said something then, Danny, about hiring a passage for Eily in an American vessel?'

Danny had stared at him, not knowing what to reply. That day on the Purple Mountain Hardress had half-choked him for his suggestions, and he was too cautious to risk being throttled a second time.

'Do you remember, Danny, you asked me for my glove as a token of my approval?' Hardress said. 'Well, here it is. My mind has altered. I married too young. You, Danny, were the wise one.'

Danny had taken the glove in silence.

'You shall have money,' Hardress had continued, parting with his purse. 'My wish is this. Eily must not live in Ireland. Don't take her to her father. The old man would babble, and everybody would hear about it. Three thousand miles of a roaring ocean would be a better security for silence. She must not stay in Ireland, and never let me see her more. But don't harm a hair of her head. Do you hear?'

'Oh, then, I'd do more than that for your honour,' Danny had assured him.

'When will you be returning to the cottage?'

'In a few days, sir.'

'Here, then, is a letter telling Eily that you will take her to her father. Give it to her immediately you reach the cottage,' Hardress ordered.

'I will, sir. I'll do that, sir,' Danny had promised, as Hardress had hurried from the room.

Now Eily and Danny were gone and Hardress stood in Phil Naughten's kitchen, his mind deep in trouble. He gave his great-coat to Poll, and she hung it near the fire to dry. He sat in a chair and, without speaking, gazed fixedly upon the burning embers. Then his head fell upon his breast, and he was asleep.

Poll and her husband resumed their meal, and afterwards employed themselves repairing the pony's saddle. The more Poll watched Hardress as she worked, the less she liked the way things were going.

'There's something on to-night that is not right, Phil,' she whispered. 'I'm sorry now I let Eily out of the house.'

'Whisht, you foolish woman,' Phil counselled. 'What would be going on? Mind your work and don't wake the master. D'ye hear how he moans in his sleep?'

'I do,' Poll said, 'and I think that moan isn't for nothing either.'

As they watched the sleeping Hardress they noticed that his breathing was oppressed and thick, and his forehead became covered with beads of sweat.

A murmur occasionally broke from his lips, and a hurried whisper sometimes angrily in command and other times brittle with fear, would escape him.

'The Lord defend and forgive us all!' said Phil in a low voice to his wife. 'I'll judge nobody but I'm afraid there's some bad work, as you say, going on this night.'

'God protect the poor girl that left us,' whispered Poll.

'Amen!' replied Phil, aloud.

'Amen!' echoed Hardress, and following the association awakened by the response he ran over, in a rapid voice, a number of prayers such as used in the service of his church.

'He's saying his litanies,' said Poll. 'Phil, come into the next room or wake him up, either one or the other. I don't like to be listening to him. 'Tisn't right of us to be taking advantage of anybody in their dreams. Many is the poor boy that hung himself that way in his sleep.'

' 'Tis a bad business,' Phil said. 'I don't like the look of it at all, I tell you.'

'My glove! My glove!' cried the dreaming Hardress. 'You used it against my meaning. I meant but banishment. We shall both be hanged for this.'

'Come, Phil! Come out of here!' Poll said with impatience.

'Stop, eroo, stop!' Phil ordered. 'He's choking, I believe! Poll, get a cup of water.'

'Here it is. Shake him, Phil! Master Hardress, wake up, a graw geal!'

Phil put his hand on the sleeping man's shoulder.

'Wake, Master Hardress! Wake up, sir, if you please!'

The instant he was touched Hardress sprang from the chair and remained standing before the fire, his eyes wide with fear. Then, hurrying from the cottage, he ran down the crags, leaving Poll at the door watching after him with his great-coat in her hands.

When he went into the house his mother had news for him. Mrs. Daly, a friend of the family, had died and they were to start off at daybreak for Limerick to attend the funeral.

'It is a long distance,' Hardress told her, 'but I can be there by nightfall. When does the funeral take place?'

'After to-morrow, I suppose,' his mother said. 'I will have the curricle at the door by daybreak, for you must set me down at Anne Chute's home. With your marriage to her fixed for the second of February, there are a lot of things to be arranged. Go now and change your wet clothes or you will suffer for it. Nancy shall take you a warm foot-bath and a hot drink when you are in your room.'

All night long Hardress tossed in his bed, and whenever his eyes closed a chain of faces passed before his imagination, some of them threatening him and the others deriding. His love for Anne Chute now took second place in his mind to his uncertainty about Eily's fate at the hands of Danny Mann, and he was possessed by remorse. When the dreary winter dawn lightened the bedroom he was still unrefreshed and feverish.

He arose and found his mother dressed for the journey. They took a hurried breakfast by candlelight, while the groom was tackling the horse to the curricle. As they drove away, the lakes were still covered by a low mist which concealed the islands and the distant shores, and magnified the height of the gigantic mountains by which the waters are walled in.

About noon they stopped to eat and hear Mass at the town of Listowel. Mrs. Cregan and her son were shown into the parlour at the inn, the window of which looked out upon the square. The bell of the Chapel on the other side was ringing for last Mass, which they attended. When they had returned to the inn Mrs. Cregan stared hard at Hardress.

'Do you intend to call in at Castle Chute to see Anne?'

'Just for a few moments,' Hardress told her.

'In that case I would advise you to do something about your appearance,' Mrs. Cregan said. 'You look a perfect fright.'

He looked in the mirror and saw that his mother's description was not exaggerated. His eyes were bloodshot, his beard grown and grizzly, and his hair was badly in need of trimming. He rang the small bell and the landlady came. It would be difficult, she told him, today being a holiday, to get a hair-cutter, but there was one from Garryowen below in the kitchen who could do the business as good as the best if he had only got his scissors with him.

The hair-cutter was a small, thin-faced, red-haired man with a tailor's shears dangling from his finger. He entered the room, bowing and smiling with a timid and conciliating air.

'The potatoes were very early this year, sir,' he modestly began, after he had wrapped a check apron about the neck of Hardress. 'Very early, sir. The white-eyes especially. For the first four months I wouldn't ask a better potato than the white-eye, with a bit of bacon if one had it. But after that the meal goes out of them and they gets wet and bad. Turn your head more to the light, sir, if you please.'

'You needn't cut so fast,' Hardress, who was in no mood to receive a lecture on the virtues of the potato, told him.

'Slender food the potato is indeed,' the hair-cutter continued.

'There's a deal of poor people here in Ireland, sir, that are run so hard at times, that the wind of a bit of meat is as good to them as the meat itself to those that would be used to it. The potatoes are everything. But there's a sort of potato, I don't know did your honour ever taste them, and 'tis killing half the country. The white potato it is, that will grow in very poor land and requires but little manure. But it has no more strength and nourishment in it than if you had boiled a handful of sawdust and made gruel of it, or put a bit of a deal board between your teeth and thought to make a breakfast of it.'

He was better at talking than at hair-dressing as Hardress discovered when he consulted the mirror and saw his head cut as bare as an egg, with a narrow fringe around his forehead, like the ends of a piece of silk. It was a fashion popular with people who employed a barber three or four times a year and who believed in getting value for their money. There was no help, however, for such mischief once effected, and Hardress paid him without comment.

The little hair-cutter who had been compensated handsomely for his handiwork bowed very low as Hardress gazed mournfully at the mirror.

'If your honour would ever be passing through Garryowen, and would be inclined to leave any of your hair behind you, maybe you'd think of Dunat O'Leary's shop on the right hand side of the street, three doors from Mihil O'Connor's the ropemaker.'

'You are a bit far from your place of business, aren't you?' Hardress remarked.

'The reason that has me in Listowel, your honour,' Dunat O'Leary said, 'is in consequence of a letter I received from a neighbour's daughter that ran away from her father, and is hid somewhere among the Kerry mountains.'

'A letter *you* received?' Hardress cried in astonishment.

'Yes, sir. Telling me she was alive, and bidding me let the old man know about it. Mihil O'Connor that I mentioned a while ago. Since I came I heard it reported at Castle Island this morning that they thought she was drowned somewhere in the Flesk.'

'Drowned! Eily drowned!' Hardress suddenly exclaimed, his eyes widening with fear.

'Eily was her name, sure enough,' the barber said, staring at him. 'How did you come to know it?'

Hardress covered up the slip of the tongue as well as he could.

You mentioned that name, I think. Did you not?'

'Maybe, it slipped from me, sir. Well, as I was saying, they thought she was drowned there, and they were for having a sheaf of reeds with her name tied upon it put out upon the stream; for they say that when a person dies by water the sheaf of reeds will float against the stream or with the stream, until it stops over the place where the body lies, if it had to go up O'Sullivan's cascade itself. But Father Edward O'Connor desired them to go home about their business, that the sheaf would go with the current and no way else, if they were at it from this till doomsday. To be sure he knew best.'

At this moment the landlady knocked at the door to tell Hardress that Mrs. Cregan was anxious to continue the journey. He hurried out of the room to join his mother, glad of his release from the wondering eyes of the hair-cutter, and at a moment when he felt his agitation increasing so fast that it threatened to overwhelm him.

🪶 7 *At Mrs. Daly's Wake*

WHEN HARDRESS ENTERED MR. DALY'S HOUSE to attend the wake he was shown into the parlour, in which the gentlemen were seated round the fire, and listening to the sounds of mourning coming from the room where the body of Mrs. Daly, who had died in childbirth, was laid out. The table was covered with decanters of wine, bowls of whiskey-punch, and long glasses. A big turf fire blazed in the grate, and Lowry Looby was placing on the table a pair of plated candlesticks almost as long as himself. Mr. Cregan, father of Hardress, his friend, Mr. Connolly, Doctor Leake and several other gentlemen were seated at one side of the fire. The others in the parlour were family connections, their tradesmen, and some of the more comfortable class of tenants. One or two persons attended to the company, supplying them with liquor, and making punch according as the fountain was exhausted.

When Hardress appeared at the door his eye met Connolly, who beckoned to him and made room for him upon his own chair. Lowry Looby handed him a cup of tea and he was sipping it in silence when a slight touch on his arm made him turn around. He saw behind him an old man dressed in dark frieze, with both hands crossed on the head of his walking-stick, his chin resting upon them, watching him. It was Eily's father, Mihil O'Connor, the rope-maker.

'I beg your pardon, sir,' Mihil said gently, 'but I think I have seen your face somewhere before now. Did you ever spend an evening at Garryowen?"

Hardress said nothing but stared at him in silence.

'Don't you remember, sir, on a Patrick's eve, saving an old man and a girl from a parcel of the boys in Mungret Street?' Old Mihil asked.

'I do,' Hardress answered in a low, hoarse voice.

'I thought I remembered the face, and the make,' Mihil said. 'Well, sir, I'm the same old man, and many's the time since that night that I wished both she and myself had died in that spot together.'

'I pity you,' muttered Hardress. 'I pity you, although you may not think it.'

'The girl you saw that night with me, she was a beautiful little girl, sir, wasn't she?' the old man asked.

'Do you think so?' Hardress murmured stupidly.

'Do I think so?' echoed the father with a grim smile. 'It's little matter what her father thought. The world knew her for a beauty, but what was the good of it? She left me there and went off with a stranger.'

Hardress again said something, but it resembled only the delirious murmurs of a person on the rack.

'I'm ashamed of myself to be always this way,' continued Mihil. 'I'm like an old woman, moaning and ochoning among the neighbours. I'm like an old goose that would be cackling after the flock, or a fool of a little bird whistling upon a bough of a summer evening, after the nest is robbed.'

'How close this room is!' Hardress said. 'The heat is suffocating.'

'I thought at first that it is dead she was,' Mihil told him. 'But then a letter come to a neighbour of mine to let me know she was alive and hearty. I know how it was. Some villain that enticed her off. I sent the neighbour westwards to look after her, and I thought he'd be back today but he isn't. I told him to call to my brother, the priest, in Castle Island. Sure, he writes me word he seen her of a Christmas Day last, and that she told him she was married, and coming home shortly. Aye, I'm afraid the villain deceived her and that she's not rightly married, for I made it my business to inquire of every priest in town and country, and none of them could tell me a word about it. She deceived me, and I'm afraid he's deceiving her. There, let him! There, let him! But there's a throne in heaven, and there's One upon it, and that man, and my daughter, and myself will stand together before that throne one day!'

Hardress could control his feelings no longer.

'Let me go!' he cried aloud, and breaking violently from the circle. 'Let me go! My God, can anyone bear this?'

He struggled through the astonished crowd and went out the door.

'He's a good young gentleman,' Mihil O'Connor said, looking after him, and addressing those who sat around. 'He's a kind young gentleman. Mind you, he has great nature in him.'

Lowry Looby removed the tea-service from the parlour, and took his seat on a chair before the kitchen fire. The kitchen was also crowded with mourners. On a wooden form at one side were seated the female servants of the house, and opposite them the hearse-driver, the mutes, the drivers of the hack-carriages, and some gentlemen's servants. A table was covered with bread, jugs of punch, and Cork porter.

' 'Twill be a good funeral,' said the hearse-driver, laying aside the mug of porter, from which he had just taken a refreshing swig.

'If it isn't, it ought,' said Lowry. 'They're people, sir, that are well-known in the country.'

'And well-liked, too, by all accounts,' one of the hack-coachmen declared.

A moan from all the women showed that the accounts were correct.

'Ah, she was a queen of a little woman,' Lowry said. 'She was too good for this world. Oh, vo, where's the use of talking at all! Sure 'twas only a few days since I was salting the bacon at the table over, and she standing near me, knitting. Little I thought that she wouldn't live to taste a rasher of it.'

A pause of deep affliction followed this speech, which was broken by the hearse-driver.

'The grandest funeral that ever I saw in my life was that of the Marquis of Waterford, father of the present man. It was a sight for a king. There were six men marching out before the hearse, with gold sticks in their hands, and as much black silk about them as a lady. The coffin was covered all over with black velvet and gold, and there was his name above upon the top of it, on a great gold plate entirely, that was shining like the sun. I never seen such a sight before nor since. There was forty-six carriages after the hearse, and every one of them belonging to a lord, or an estated man at the least. It flogged all the shows I ever see since I was able to walk the ground.'

Lowry, who felt that poor Mrs. Daly's funeral must necessarily shrink into insignificance in comparison with this magnificent description, let loose a few philosophical remarks upon the company.

'The Lord save us, it isn't what gold they had upon their hearses they'll be asked where they are going, only what use they made of the gold and silver that was given them in this world. 'Tisn't how they were buried, they'll be asked, but how they lived. And them are the questions Mrs. Daly could answer this night as well as the Marquis of Waterford, or any other lord or marquis in the land.'

Lowry's philosophy won over the company. The procession of the marquis, the gold sticks, the silks, the velvet, and the forty-six carriages were forgotten. The hearse-driver buried his face in his mug of good Cork porter, and the remainder of the mourners returned to their attitudes of silence and dejection.

8 Murder Will Out

THE MARRIAGE of Hardress Cregan and Anne Chute was postponed for some time over the death of Mrs. Daly, who had been a friend of both families. Nothing, in the meantime, was heard of Eily or Danny Mann, and the remorse and suspense endured by Hardress began to affect his mind and health so much that Anne Chute and Mrs. Cregan grew alarmed. His manner to Anne changed almost hourly. On the one hand he was tender, passionate, and full of affection, and without warning he could become sullen, curt, intemperate and gloomy. His frequent unkindness caused her pain, but she put his moods down to a bout of bad health which she hoped would cure in time.

Mrs. Cregan was more deeply worried. With a mother's keener eye she saw that Hardress had done something to affect his conscience, and she gathered, without learning the full truth, that her son had put himself within the power of outraged justice. From the moment of this discovery she, too, became subject to fits of abstraction and of unusual seriousness in her daily dealings with people.

One morning, three weeks after Eily's disappearance, and in the hope that it would keep his mind from thinking upon her, Hardress rode out to hunt the fox with Hepton Connolly, and some other gentlemen. The fox was said to have his earth in the side of a hill, near the river, which on one side was grey with limestone crags, and on the other covered with a quantity of short furze. Towards the water a wet winding path among the underwood led downward to a large marsh which lay close to the shore. It was overgrown with short rushes, and intersected with little creeks and channels which were filled only when the spring-tide was at the full.

The search after the fox continued for a long time without any success, and the gentlemen became impatient and cocked worried eyes at the heavy sky.

'No fox to-day, I fear,' said Mr. Cregan, riding up to join his son and Hepton Connolly. 'I hope dinner has been ordered early, for I don't think we'll be late for it.'

Mr. Connolly stood in his stirrups and looked towards the river.

'Something stirring at last,' he said. 'What are the hounds doing now?'

'They have left the cover on the hill and are trying the marsh,' cried a gentleman who was galloping past.

'The dogs are chopping,' Connolly said. 'They have found Reynard. Come away!'

''Tis a false scent,' declared an elderly huntsman. ''Ware hare!'

''Ware hare!' was shouted by many voices, and the crowd upon the brow of the hill hurried down to the marsh.

'There is something extraordinary happening,' Mr.

Cregan said. 'What makes all the crowd collect upon the marsh?'

As Hardress watched the crowd he was filled with uneasiness. The hounds were baying loudly as if they had found a strong scent, and yet there was no sign of the fox appearing.

A horseman left the crowd on the marsh and galloped towards them, and when he approached Hardress observed the expression of fear and pity on his face.

'Mr. Warner, I believe you are a magistrate,' he said to the elderly huntsman.

Mr. Warner bowed.

'Then come this way, sir, if you please. Something terrible has happened.'

'No harm to any of our friends, I hope,' Mr. Warner said, putting spurs to his horse.

The answer of the stranger was lost in the tramp of the hooves as they rode away.

Immediately afterwards two other horsemen came galloping by. One of them held in his hand a straw bonnet beaten out of shape and stained with the black mire of the marsh. Hardress heard him say 'horrible' as they rode swiftly past.

'What's horrible?' Hardress shouted, rising in his stirrups.

But the two horsemen were already out of hearing, and he looked at his father and Mr. Connolly.

'What does he call horrible?' he asked them.

'I couldn't tell you,' Connolly said. 'Come down to the marsh and we'll find out.'

In the marsh a dense crowd was collected around one of the little channels, and the whipper-in was flogging the curious hounds away from it.

'Bad luck to ye, what a fox ye found for us this morning!' Hardress heard him exclaim as he passed. 'How bad ye are now for a taste of Christian's flesh!'

Hardress dismounted and pushed his way into the centre of the ring. Here he stopped short and gazed in horror upon the picture which the crowd had concealed from him. On a bank beside him lay an object, concealed for the most part beneath a large blue mantle. A pair of small feet, in Spanish-leather shoes, appeared from below the end of the garment, and a mass of long fair hair escaped from beneath the capacious hood. It was the body of his wife.

Beyond the crowd the hounds began to bay loudly again. Hardress started from his posture of rigid horror, and burst into a passion of wild fear.

'The hounds!' he shouted. 'Mr. Warner, do you hear them? Keep off the hounds. They will tear her to pieces if you let them pass!'

'There is no fear of that happening,' Warner said, fixing a keen eye upon him.

'And I tell you there is,' Hardress cried. 'Good God, sir, will you allow the dogs to tear her? Do you not hear them yelling for blood? You are at liberty to contradict me by virtue of your office but I have my remedy. You can expect to hear further from me.'

Forcing his way violently through the crowd, Hardress vaulted into the saddle and galloped, as if he were on a steeple-chase, in the direction of Castle Chute.

'If you are a gentleman,' Magistrate Warner remarked, looking after Hardress, 'you are as ill-tempered a gentleman as ever I met, or something a great deal worse.'

Oblivious to it all, Eily O'Connor Cregan lay sodden and silent in her blue cloak, waiting for someone to put a name on her.

※ 9 Danny is Captured

MRS. CREGAN, who with her husband and son was staying in Castle Chute, had a mind not to be envied by anyone with the power to know the load it carried. On his return home from the hunt Hardress had confessed his sordid part in the murder of Eily to her, an admission which, understandably, had her in a dead faint at his feet. Now the net was tightening but there was a hope that her son would not be called upon to pay the penalty for his crime. Eily's body had been identified; Lowry Looby's letter revealed that she had been lodging with the Naughtens, and there was a hue and cry for Danny Mann, who had disappeared. Hardress thought that Danny had gone to America, and if this was correct the only people who could give evidence of Eily's association with Hardress were the Naughtens. Mrs. Cregan believed that money would seal the lips of Poll and Phil quite effectively. She was turning the whole painful business over in her mind when a servant arrived to inform her that she was wanted in the ballroom.

When she reached the narrow hall near the entrance her eyes widened. Close to the wall on either side a number of soldiers with shining muskets were standing stiffly, like the wax figures in the shop of a London tailor. Another soldier, on guard outside the ballroom, opened the door and she went in, her mind in a whirl. Around a table in the centre of the room stood Magistrate Warner, Mr. Cregan, Captain Gibson of the Army, and a clerk. At the farther end of the table stool a low squalid and ill-shaped person, his arm suspended in a cotton handkerchief, his dress covered with mud, and his face bloody. Danny Mann had delayed his flight to America too long.

Mrs. Cregan, who recognised Danny immediately, walked calmly forward with that air of easy dignity which she could assume even when her whole nature was at war within her. Mr. Warner informed her that they were awaiting the arrival of the Naughtens from Killarney. Danny had been questioned but his answers were all given in the true style of Irish witnesses when cross-examined by their English oppressors, seeming to evince the utmost frankness, yet invariably leaving the questioner in greater perplexity than before he began the examination.

While Mrs. Cregan remained there, pondering the new twist in the situation of her son's crime, a bustle was heard outside the door, and a female voice was raised high in anger and remonstrance. It was Poll of the Reeks, freshly arrived from Killarney. Poll strode into the room and burst into loud lamentation when she saw her brother.

'Danny, a graw geal! O vo, vo, vo, asthore, is that the way it is with you? What did you do to them, Danny Boy?'

'That the two hands may stick to me, Poll, if I know,' replied the prisoner. 'They say 'tis to kill someone I done. They think one Eily O'Connor was a lodger of ours westwards, and that I took her out of a night and murdered her. Isn't that purty talk? Sure you know yourself we had no lodgers.'

'Remove that prisoner,' Mr. Warner ordered. 'He must not be present at her examination.'

Danny was removed, but the harm had been done and

Poll had learned all she wanted to know. The examination of Fighting Poll began.

'Poll Naughten is your name, is it not?'

'Polly Mann they christened me for want of a better, and for want of a worse I took up with Naughten.'

'You live in the Gap of Dunloe?'

'Yes, when at home.'

'Did you know the deceased, Eily O'Connor?'

'I never knew a girl of that name.'

'Take care of your answers. We have strong evidence.'

'If you have it as strong as a cable you can make the most of it. You have my answer.'

'Do you remember a man named Looby being in your house last autumn?'

'I do well.'

'Did you give him a letter on that evening?'

'He made more free than welcome. I can tell him that.'

'Answer my question. Did you give him a letter?'

'Many's the thing I gave him and I'm sorry I didn't give him a thing more along with them, and that's a good flaking.'

'Answer my question. Did you give Looby a letter?'

'Listen to me now, please, your honour. That the head may go to the grave with me——"

'Did you give Looby the letter?'

'As sure as I'm upon my oath, I never swopped a word with Lowry Looby from that day to this.'

'Whew!' said the magistrate, 'there's an answer. I ask you once again did you give Looby a letter?'

'Does Lowry say I gave him a letter?'

'Woman,' Mr. Warner told her, 'remember that you have sworn to tell the whole truth.'

'Sure, it's the whole truth I'm telling and ye won't listen to half of it,' Poll parried.

'Go on,' said the magistrate with a deep sigh.

'I say this, sir, and I'll stand to it. Looby gave me impudence and I did give him a stroke or two. Let him make the most of it. I did. I admit it.'

'And after the strokes you gave Looby a letter?'

'What letter?'

Mr. Warner knew when he was beaten.

'Take that woman into another room and bring up Philip Naughten,' he ordered.

Complaining loudly that she had been insulted and ill-treated, Poll was removed. Her husband was next admitted and he approached the table with a fawning smile upon his face, and a helpless, conciliating glance at every individual around him.

'Now we shall get somewhere,' the magistrate congratulated himself upon having a simple honest fellow before him at last. "Your name is Philip Naughten, is it not?'

Phil let loose a flood of Irish which the magistrate cut short without delay.

'Answer me in English, friend. We speak no Irish here. Can you speak English, fellow?'

'Not a word, please your honour.'

A roar of laughter from the listeners greeted this admission, and Phil listened to it with a wondering and stupid look. Then turning to Mr. Cregan, he addressed him at some length in Irish.

'He says he does not know enough English to make himself clear,' Mr. Cregan explained.

'Then, I suppose, we must have the business in Irish,' the magistrate decided. 'Mr. Dawly will act as interpreter.'

For all the worthwhile information he got, Mr. Dawley might as well have been listening to Hindustani. Phil received the questions with a plodding, meditative look, and answered with a countenance of honest grief and an apparent anxiety to be understood, which would have baffled the penetration of anyone not a practised observer. So earnest was his manner that Mr. Warner believed he was returning satisfactory answers.

If it was Poll's policy to admit very little, it seemed to be the policy of her husband to give no information at all.

Did he know Eily O'Connor?

Phil gaped upon the interpreter in silence for some moments, and then looked at the magistrate as if to gather the meaning of the question.

'Repeat it for him,' Mr. Warner ordered.

Dan Dawley did so.

' 'Tis the answer he makes me, your honour, that he's a poor man that lives by industrying.'

'Did he know Eily O'Connor?'

When he was a young man he rented a small farm from Mr. O'Connor of Cra-beg, near Tralee, Phil admitted.

He looked at the magistrate with a simple smile as

though he expected to get a fist of silver for supplying this information.

Threats, promises of favour, adroit questions were used to draw from him the frankness which was desired, but he remained adamant. He would admit nothing more than that he was a poor man who lived by his industry, and that he had rented a small farm from Mr. O'Connor of Cra-beg, near Tralee. Nothing more could be done until fresh, and more honest, witnesses arrived to give their testimony. Separate places of confinement were allotted to the three prisoners, a sentinel was placed over each, the gentlemen adjourned to the consolations of Castle Chute's dining-parlour, and the soldiers were entertained like princes in the servants' hall.

🕸 10 A Ghost is Seen

THE PLACE IN which Danny Mann was confined had been a stable, but it had fallen into decay and was now no longer in use. The rack and manger were still attached to the wall, and a space in the roof let in the moonlight. Danny sat warming his fingers over a small fire heaped against the wall, and listened to the sentinel marching up and down outside the stable-door. Then, pulling a roast potato from the embers, he was about to eat his frugal supper when a noise at the window sent him creeping softly into a dark corner of the stable. The shutters of the window were opened with great caution, a figure wrapped in a white sheet entered quietly, the shutters were closed again and the visitor stood before the fire, his eyes searching the darkness for the prisoner. It was Hardress Cregan, and Danny's eyes filled with tears as he saw how much for the worse his master had changed since the carefree days of not so long ago.

'Master Hardress,' he said, 'is it you I see that way?'

'Where is Eily?' murmured Hardress, drawing the sheet around his head, and then falling into a silence broken now and again by moans of deep agony.

Danny sank trembling on his knees, and responded to them with tears and sobs.

'Master Hardress, if there's anything I can do to make your mind easy, say the word. And if they find me out itself they'll never be one straw the wiser of who advised me to do it. They may hang me as high as they please, they may flake the life out of me but I'll never tell them what it was made me do it.'

'Quiet, you hypocrite!' Hardress ordered. 'All the years I have heaped kindnesses upon you and this is how you have repaid me.'

Danny gaped at his master, for a reproach was the last thing he expected from him.

'There are some people that are hard to please, Master Hardress, and you seem to be one of them. Do you remember saying anything to me in the room in Killarney? Do you remember giving me a glove at all? I had my token surely for what I done.'

He drew the glove from his pocket and held it out to Hardress who waved it away with disgust.

'I thought I had ears to hear that time, and brains to understand,' Danny continued. 'I'm sure it was no benefit to me that there should be a hue-and-cry over the mountains after a lost lady, and a chance of a hempen cravat for my trouble. But I had my warrant. That was your very word, Master Hardress. *'When you go here is your warrant,'* says you, and you gave me the glove. Weren't them your words?'

'But not for death,' Hardress cried. 'I did not say for death.'

'I own you didn't,' returned Danny, who was angered by what he considered a shuffling attempt to escape out of the transaction. 'I own you didn't. I felt for you, and I wouldn't wait for you to say it. But did you mean it?'

'No!' Hardress exclaimed. 'I did not mean you to take her life. As I hope to meet Eily before God, I did not. I even bade you to avoid it. I warned you not to touch her.'

'You did,' Danny said, 'and your eye looked murder while you said it. After this I won't ever again look in any man's face to know what he means. But listen to me, Master Hardress. As sure as that fire there is burning, the sign of death was on your face that time, whatever way your words went.'

'From what could you gather it?' Hardress asked.

'From what? From everything. Listen hither. Didn't you remind me then of my own offer on the Purple Mountain a while before, and tell me if I was to make that offer again you'd think different? And didn't you give me the glove you refused me then? Ah, this is what makes me sick, after I putting my head into the halter for a man. And now to call me out of my name, and to tell me I done it for harm. Dear knows, it wasn't for any good I hoped for it, here or hereafter, or for any pleasure I took in it, that it was done. And talking of hereafter, Master Hardress, listen to me. Eily O'Connor is in heaven and she has told her story. There are two books kept up there, they tell us, of all our doings, good and bad. And take my word for this, in which-ever of them books my name is wrote, your own name is not far from it.'

Outside, the sentry stopped beside the door and listened.

'Is everything all right in there?' he called out.

'All's right *your* way, but not *my* way,' returned Danny, sulkily.

The sentry shouldered his musket and resumed his walk, humming a song to shorten the hours.

Hardress turned to Danny and looked hard at him a few moments.

'We won't argue any more about it, Danny; the time is running out. Tell me this. If I help you to escape, will you promise to leave the country at once?'

Danny's eyes sparkled in the firelight.

'Do you think a fox would refuse to run to earth with the hounds at his brush? Danny's no fool, you know.'

'Here then,' Hardress said, putting a purse of money in his hand. 'This window here is unguarded. There is a path through the hay-yard, and then cross the field in the direction of the road. Go at once.'

'What about the sentry? He'll be around shouting his question in a couple of minutes.'

'I will stay here and answer until you have had time to escape,' Hardress promised. 'Take the road to Cork where you will be sure to find vessels ready to sail. If ever I find you on Irish soil again, I will kill you!'

'And is this the way we part after all!' Danny sorrowed. 'Well, then, be it so. Perhaps, after you think longer of it Master, you may think better of me.'

And, going out the window with the agility of a monkey, he disappeared into the night.

Hardress remained for a considerable time leaning

against the wall, and gazing with a vacant eye upon the dying fire. The sentinel challenged several times, and seemed well content with the answers he received. Eventually Hardress became so absorbed in his thoughts that he failed to hear the soldier's challenge. Becoming alarmed, the man opened the door and looked in. Instead of his little prisoner he saw to his astonishment a tall figure wrapped in white, and a ghastly face on which the embers of the fire shed a dreary light. Like many a good soldier before and after him, he believed in ghosts and this was the nearest he had ever come to meeting with one. He found enough strength to fire his musket in alarm before he fell senseless on the stones of the yard. Hardress, no less frightened than the soldier, slipped swiftly out the window and hurried to his room.

When the soldiers answered the alarm, they found the sentinel lying senseless across the stock of his musket, the stable-door open, and the prisoner vanished. When the sentinel recovered, his strange story was in some degree confirmed by one of his comrades, who stated that he saw a tall white figure gliding among the haystacks where it changed into the shape of a red heifer, a tribute to the excellent entertainment he was receiving in the servants' hall.

The story that ran through the countryside the following day was an improvement on the original. It was whispered that the ghost of Eily O'Connor had appeared to the sentinel to declare Danny Mann's innocence and to demand that he be set free. The unfortunate sentry was placed under close arrest until Captain Gibson thought up a sufficient punishment to fit his crime. As the worthy Captain did not believe in ghosts, either Irish or English, it was expected that the punishment would be a severe one.

With Danny vanished the case against Poll and Phil Naughten collapsed. If they were cautious in their admissions while he was in custody, they became completely tongue-tied when they heard of his escape. Magistrate Warner, who hoped he would never look upon, or have to listen to, their likes again, sent them back to their cottage in Killarney where, no doubt, the full powers of their speech were soon restored to them.

🌿 *11 Danny's Revenge*

NOTWITHSTANDING THE ASSURANCES OF DANNY that he
would put a few thousand miles of water between himself
and the hangman, Hardress was worried. It was an even
chance that Danny, with money to burn, was risking the
chances of detection for the rare satisfaction of playing
host to his cronies in the taverns of Limerick. Hardress
had grown up with Danny and knew that what he said
he'd do was often different to what he did. In the vernac-
ular of his native county, Danny would promise you Abbey-
dorney and he'd give you Ardfert. But Hardress arrived
at the truth of the matter sooner than he expected.

He was walking with Anne along the sea-road beside
Castle Chute when they saw and heard the May Day
mummers approaching. Young men with painted faces,
ribbon-bright hats, sashes, musical instruments, long poles
with handkerchiefs fluttering at the top, marched merrily
along to welcome the summer in. Behind and on each side
were a number of boys and girls, adding their shrill voices
to the confusion.

They came to a halt and formed a semi-circle across
the road as Anne and Hardress came in sight. The musicians struck up a jig and one of the young men pulled a girl
from the crowd and began to dance. After the custom of
the countryside Hardress was compelled, much against his
will, to dance with the same girl when the young man had
finished his jig. Afterwards he was expected to show his
appreciation of the honour done him, by dropping something handsome into the piper's hat.

While he was dancing, Anne strolled on alone. Suddenly
the music stopped and she turned. She saw Hardress in
the middle of the mummers, gripping one of them by the
throat and then throwing him violently against the dry-
stone wall on the far side of the road. The man rose again
and, looking after Hardress, tossed his hand above his head
and shook it in a menacing manner.

Hardress hurried away from the group, many of whom
were gazing after him in astonishment, while others gathered around the injured man as they inquired the cause
of the singular and unprovoked assault. The same inquiry

was made by Anne who was astonished at the change in her lover's appearance. Hardress made some confused and unsatisfactory answer, talked of the fellow's insolence and his own warm temper, and they hurried back to the quietness of Castle Chute by another road.

The wedding-feast for Anne and Hardress was appointed for the evening of the following day, and the ceremony itself was to take place early on the morning after this entertainment, the honeymoon to be spent in the south of France. Before sunset the Castle was crowded with blue coats and snow-white silks. Bonfires were lighted on the road before the avenue gate, and in front of each public-house in the neighbourhood, for Anne was a popular young lady with everybody. The little village was illuminated and bands of rural musicians, followed by crowds of merry idlers, strolled up and down playing various lively airs, and often halting to partake of the refreshments which were free and plentiful to all who chose to draw upon the hospitality of the Chute family.

While Castle Chute and its vicinity were making merry, Magistrate Warner was quietly enjoying a bowl of punch in his house eight miles away, with Captain Gibson and Mr. Houlahan, the clerk, for company. Their leisure was interrupted by a servant coming in and telling the magistrate that a stranger wished to speak to him on judicial business.

'Pooh,' said Mr. Warner, 'some broken head or sixpenny summons. Let him come back tomorrow morning.'

'He says his business is very pressing, sir, and 'twill be more your own loss than his if you let him go,' the servant replied.

'In that case we must hear him. Captain Gibson, I know you find these examinations amusing. Shall I have him in here?'

'You could not do me a greater pleasure,' the Captain said. 'These people are the only actors on earth.'

The stranger was shown in and his story seemed to be almost told by his appearance, for one of his eyes was blackened and puffed out, so as nearly to disguise the entire countenance.

'Well, my good man, what is your business with me?' Mr. Warner asked.

'I'm not a good man, as my business with you will show,'

the stranger replied. 'Aren't you the coroner that sat upon Eily O'Connor?'

'I am.'

'Did you find the murderers yet?'

'They are not in custody, but we have strong information.'

'Then, listen to me and I'll make it strong enough for you,' the stranger said.

'This instant,' replied Mr. Warner. 'Mr. Houlahan, take down this examination.'

'Do,' said the stranger. 'Put every sentence in your book, for every word I have to say is gold to you and to the counsellors. And write down first that Eily O'Connor was surely murdered, and that I, Danny Mann, was the one that done the deed.'

'Mann!' exclaimed the magistrate. 'Our fugitive prisoner?'

'I was your prisoner till I was set at liberty by one that had reason for doing it. I'm now come to deliver myself up and to tell the whole truth, for I'm tired of my life.'

Mr. Warner paused for a moment in strong amazement.

'I must warn you that your confession will not entitle you to mercy, and it will be used in evidence against yourself,' he told Danny.

'It was not the fear of death or the hope of pardon that brought me here, but because I was deceived and disappointed in one that I thought more of than of my own life,' Danny replied bitterly. 'Do you see this hump on my back? All my days that was my curse. In place of being, as I ought to be, fighting at the fair, drinking at the wake, and dancing in the jighouse, there's the figure I cut all my days. And who have I to thank for that? Mr. Hardress Cregan. 'Twas he that done it to me and I a little boy. In spite of it I loved him, but what's the use of talking? He met me yesterday upon the road and what did he do? He struck me, he called me out of my name, and then he flung me back against the wall, just the same way as when he hurted my back long ago and made me a cripple for life. He doesn't feel for me and I won't feel for him. He had his revenge and now I'll have mine. Write down Danny Mann for the murderer of Eily, and write down Hardress Cregan for his adviser.'

His listeners started and looked at one another.

'Well ye may start,' Danny told them. 'But I have witnesses for ye. Eily O'Connor was Hardress Cregan's wife. Ye start at that bit of news too. There's the certificate of her marriage. Write down that in your book, and write down Phil Naughten and his wife for having Eily in their house. Put down Lowry Looby after, and then Myles Na Gopaleen Murphy, and Mihil O'Connor, the father.'

Mr. Warner jumped up from his seat.

'Mr. Houlahan, lock up the prisoner. Come, Captain Gibson, we will ride for a guard to your quarters and then proceed to arrest Cregan. I am sorry for it. 'Tis a shocking business.'

'We must proceed with great delicacy, sir,' Captain Gibson advised. 'So amiable a family, and such a shock to them.'

They rode rapidly away, collected their guard of soldiers and soon were galloping up to the open hospitable doors of Castle Chute. They arrested Hardress and went into the night, leaving behind them a delirious Mrs. Cregan, her drunken husband in the middle of his drunken cronies, and a bewildered Anne Chute. Captain Gibson was worried in case someone might attempt a rescue, but the whole business had been conducted with so much rapidity that the circumstances of Hardress Cregan's capture were not generally known, even in the Castle, for some time after his departure.

It only remains for us to inform the reader, in general terms, of the subsequent fortunes of the various actors in this domestic drama.

Hardress Cregan's life was spared, and he was sentenced to quit the shores of Ireland for ever. On the day the convict-ship sailed out of Limerick with him, Mihil O'Connor was buried in Mungret graveyard with Eily.

Danny Mann was hanged and he died amid all the agonies of a remorse, which made even those whose eyes had often looked upon such scenes shrink back with fear and wonder.

Mrs. Cregan lived to a ripe old age in the practice of austere and humiliating works of piety, and she became more loved among her friends and dependants than in her days of pride and haughtier influence.

Lowry Looby found himself a good wife and a freehold cottage in his native county of Clare, where he became a popular figure, puffing his pipe and entertaining his neighbours with his great fund of philosophical eloquence.

It was some years before Anne Chute recovered from the harsh blow which fate had dealt her. She then married Mr. Daly's son, Kyrle, who had been at school with Hardress. Kyrle had always been in love with her and had entertained the highest of hopes until Hardress came along to sweep her off her feet.

It was a very happy union and they lived long after in the practice of the duties of their place in life.

Good Reader, if you have shuddered at the excesses into which Hardress Cregan plunged, examine your own heart, and see if it hides nothing of the intellectual pride and volatile susceptibility of new impressions, which were the ruin of that young man. If, besides the amusement which these pages may have afforded, you should learn anything from such research for the avoidance of evil, or the pursuit of good, it will not be in vain that we have penned the story of *THE COLLEGIANS*.

❧ *Appendix*

The Appendix contains confidential letters from magistrates and others connected with the case, which were forwarded at the time to the authorities in Dublin. These documents were discovered only after intensive research work, and were first published in the first edition in 1953.

(By courtesy of the State Paper Office)

FROM: *J. F. FitzGerald, Knight of Glin.*
TO: *Rt. Hon. Chas. Grant, Chief Sec., Dublin Castle.*

Glin House,
14th September, 1819

Sir,

I regret being under the necessity of acquainting you with the circumstances attending a horrid murder which has been committed on the Shannon.

A few months since, a young woman named Ellen Hanley had been seduced from her friends by a man who had formerly been a Lieutenant in the Marine Service, of the name of John Scanlan.

They lived together for some time, and frequently went on the Shannon in a small boat, the property of Scanlan, who employed a man named Stephen Sullivan (alias Humphreys) as his servant and boatman.

On or about the 13th July last, Ellen Walsh, Patrick Case, John Mangan, and James Mitchell, obtained a passage from Scanlan, accompanied by Sullivan, and the young woman, from Kilrush in the county of Clare to Carrigafoyle, being on the opposite side of the Shannon, where they remained that night.

Case, Mangan, and Mitchell proceeded by land to Glin early the next morning. Ellen Walsh remained some short time with Scanlan, Sullivan, and the young woman, and, having seen them embark in their boat, went to Glin by land also. On the following morning, very early, Scanlan and Sullivan arrived at Glin, having with them the trunk containing the clothes of the young woman, who has been missing from that time up to the 6th of this month, when a body was found on the strand at Cairndotha,* on the County of Clare side of the Shannon.

A rope was found fastened round the neck, and from thence round the knees of the deceased.

On the first information, I immediately proceeded to the spot, accompanied by Major O'Dell, also a magistrate. I sent for Major Warburton, the Police Magistrate at Kilrush, and, no coroner being within reasonable distance, we held an inquisition on the body, which was fully identified by Ellen Walsh, and a verdict of wilful murder found against John Scanlan and Stephen Sullivan.

We have not yet succeeded in apprehending them, but have taken Sullivan's sister, in whose possession we found many articles, the property of the deceased. We, therefore, trust His Excellency, the Lord Lieutenant, will offer such reward as will ensure their apprehension.

*Cairndotha is another name for Moneypoint.

I also fear that I cannot obtain a sufficient recognisance to ensure the testimony of Ellen Walsh, and Mary Sullivan, on who's evidence the whole of the prosecution will rest. I therefore request that you will inform me how far I may be informed to detain them till the next Limerick Assizes.

I have the honour to be, Sir,
Your obedient servant,
J. F. FitzGerald,
Knight of Glin.

FROM: *Major Warburton, Chief of the Police in Co. Clare, and Police Magistrate.*
TO: *Rt. Hon. Chas. Grant, Chief Sec., Dublin Castle.*

Kilrush,
22nd September, 1819

Sir,
I have the honour to acknowledge the receipt of your letter of the 17th inst., and to state that every exertion has been made to apprehend Sullivan, who came to this county after the inquest.

I have received information that he went to Galway, and I have communicated with the Mayor of that town on the subject. I also received information that Scanlan was gone to Cork and I wrote to the Mayor there also.

If they are not apprehended soon, I think that a reward in the *Hue and Cry* and a description of their persons will be the most likely to succeed.

I have the honour to be, Sir,
Your most obedient humble servant,
George Warburton,
Chief Magistrate.

FROM: *J. F. FitzGerald, Knight of Glin*
TO: *Rt. Hon. Chas. Grant, Chief Sec., Dublin Castle.*

Glin House,
7th October, 1819

Sir,
I have the honour to enclose a description* of John Scanlan and Stephen Sullivan. No such description has been set on foot by the gentlemen of the country—I believe from motives of delicacy to Scanlan's family, who are highly respectable.

*The description was detached and is not available.

I cannot neglect the present opportunity of informing you that this part of the country has been in a state of ferment, in consequence of several nightly meetings, consisting of very considerable numbers, which have taken place, and from the idea of a general Rising, which is extremely prevalent with the lower orders.

We are totally destitute of military aid, and have no effective police to check their proceedings. The people are perfectly ripe for any outrage which it may be in their power to commit.

I have the honour to be, Sir
Your obedient servant,
J. F. FitzGerald,
Knight of Glin.

FROM: *Thomas Spring Rice.*
TO: *Rt. Hon. Chas Grant, Chief Sec., Dublin Castle.*

Dromoland, Ennis,
27th October, 1819

Sir,
Your are, of course, aware of the horrible murder which has lately been perpetrated on the Shannon, by two men of the names of Scanlan and Sullivan. The inquisition has probably been laid before you.

I have just received information where they are to be found; but it will require great discretion, firmness and ability to secure them. You are also probably aware that connected, as these offenders are, with some of the most powerful families in the county, the ordinary course of proceeding will with difficulty be pursued.

Men, even of independent minds, will shrink from the performance of their magisterial duty when it calls upon them to inflict sorrow and disgrace upon the families of their friends and neighbours. All the habits, most of the faults, and some of the merits of our national character, interfere with and embarrass our proceedings on this occasion.

In making this communication, I wish to submit it to your better judgment whether Major Warburton, whose zeal and ability have been so strongly shown in the police of Clare, might not be entrusted with the duty. I have written him a report on the subject, but he may, perhaps, find some difficulty in acting out of his own district.

If there are no better means of effecting the object, I shall endeavour to perform the duty myself; but from a variety of causes, unnecessary here to allude to, it would be painful and injurious to me to do so.

I shall return to Limerick tomorrow, where, should you favour me with a reply, I shall receive your letter.

I have the honour to be, Sir,

Your very obedient, very humble servant,
Thomas Spring Rice.

FROM: *Thomas Spring Rice.*
TO: *Under Sec., Wm. Gregory, Dublin Castle.*

Mount Trenchard,
Shanagolden,
22nd November, 1819

Sir,

I have the honour to enclose copies of the informations sworn against Lieutenant John Scanlan, for the murder of Ellen Hanley, a woman who lived with him.

You will perceive that the principal witness for the Crown is Ellen Walsh of Glin—this woman is now left in the country, and I very much fear that she may either be intimidated or tampered with. What I therefore take the liberty of submitting to you the propriety of sending the witness to Dublin till the Assizes, in order to ensure the production of her testimony.

Such is the condition of our county gaol, that it would be a most dangerous experiment to lodge her there, as she would be exposed to constant communication with the very persons who are most interested in suppressing her testimony.

I have the honour to be, Sir,
Your most obedient, very faithful servant,
Thomas Spring Rice.

FROM: *J. F. FitzGerald, Knight of Glin.*
TO: *Under Sec., Wm. Gregory, Dublin Castle.*

Glin House,
29th November, 1819

Sir,

I have set on foot a diligent search for Stephen Sullivan, one of the Persons concerned in the Murder of Ellen Hanley and have been successful in tracing him into a remote part of Kerry. If you could remit me a sum merely sufficient to pay the expenses of the persons I have employed, and to remunerate

them in some measure for their trouble, I am confident I shall
be enabled to apprehend him in a short time. I have the Honour
to be, Sir,

Your obedient servant,
J. F. FitzGerald.

FROM: *Henry Lyons, Magistrate, Co. Limerick.*
TO: *Under Sec., Wm. Gregory, Dublin Castle.*

Croom,
12th December, 1819

Sir,
　I have the honour to acknowledge the receipt of £10,
which I received yesterday from Major Warburton, being the
money ordered by the Lord Lieutenant to be appropriated to
the reward of the person who gave the private information which
enabled me to arrest John Scanlan, charged with the murder of
Ellen O'Donnell* on the Shannon.

I am, Sir,
Your obedient, humble servant,
Henry Lyons,
Magistrate, Co. Limerick.

*This is an obvious error for Hanley.

FROM: *Dr. McCullough (married to Scanlan's sister).*
TO: *Lord Lieutenant's Secretary, Dublin Castle.*

Bruff, Co. Limerick,
13th December, 1819

Sir,
　In consequence of a report being in circulation that I wrote
to the Castle of Dublin, to have John Scanlan taken a prisoner,
now confined in Limerick Jail for being concerned in the murder
of Ellen Hanley last July on the River Shannon, in this county,
as such a report is highly injurious to my character as a medical
man, may I request you will be pleased to contradict the same,

and have the honour to be, Sir,
your humble servant,
David McCullough, M.D., Surgeon,
and late Assistant Surgeon, 84th Regiment.

P.S.—The above mentioned culprit, I am sorry to say, is my
brother-in-law. He was a second lieutenant of Marines, was dis-

missed the Service in the month of June, 1815. After the murder of Ellen Henely—a young creature of 15 years old, whom he seduced, and took from her nearly £200, he went to Cork after robbing and murdering her, and enlisted in Captain Chitty's company, 35th Regiment, from which regiment he deserted last October, was taken prisoner on the 14th ult. at his father's, Ballycahane Castle, in this county.

The prisoner, when taken, was concealed in a bundle of straw under a manger. It was the prisoner's mother and family reported I got him taken by writing to you.

The reason of this malice to me, in circulating such reports, is on account of taking legal steps against my father-in-law, to recover £200 I entrusted to his care, which money he denied, made false reports to the Commanding Officer and Officers of my Regiment, which reports dismissed me the service, leaving me a poor wife and three helpless children in a state of starvation.

The prisoner, before he murdered her, maltreated her person, as proved before Major Odell, a magistrate for this county, together with several other crimes he committed, as proved before the coroner's inquest.

FROM: *The Right Hon. M. FitzGerald, Knight of Kerry.*
TO: *Under Sec., Wm. Gregory, Dublin Castle.*

Ballinrudery,
18th May, 1820

Dear Gregory,
      I have committed to Tralee Jail Stephen Sullivan, the associate with Scanlan, executed at the last Limerick Assizes, in the horrid murder on the Shannon.

He had concealed himself in this county for some time past, under a false name. The fellow who informed me executed the business capitally, and deserves any reward which belongs to the discovery.

Sincerely yours,
M. FitzGerald.

FROM: *The Right Hon. M. FitzGerald, Knight of Kerry.*
TO: *Under Sec., William Gregory, Dublin Castle.*

Ballinrudery,
25th May, 1820

Dear Gregory,
      Thinking twenty pounds enough for the man, I return ten, with his receipt.

It is about a month since he gave me the information first, but he suspended his proceedings till my return from a journey to Valentia. On the night of my return he apprised me that Sullivan was to be discharged from Tralee Jail on the following day, he having been sent there as a deserter.* But the fellow was early enough to anticipate his discharge. If he had got out, I am sure he would have left this country.

I fancy there are some persons speculating on getting rewards, and it seems to me the Lord Lieutenant has dealt very handsomely by Dillon.

Faithfully yours,
M. FitzGerald.

*A reference to the man who gave the information; Stephen Sullivan was in Tralee gaol on another charge.

FROM: *Francis Twiss (Magistrate), Castleisland.*
TO: *Under Sec., Wm. Gregory, Dublin Castle.*

Castleisland,
5th June, 1820

Sir,

Having heard a few days ago that the Knight of Kerry had received the reward which was offered by Government for the apprehension of a man of the name of Sullivan, who was concerned in the murder of a young woman some time back, in the County of Limerick, with a man of the name of Scanlan, who was hanged at the last Assizes of Limerick, I now beg leave to state that I am the magistrate who received the information about Sullivan, and that it was I who sent people to arrest him, and they did so, and I then had him lodged in the Gaol of Tralee, where he now is.

I therefore consider the persons I employed, together with the man who gave the information, the only persons entitled to any reward which the Government may think proper to give for his apprehension. The persons who I employed having heard that a reward was offered, have requested that I may make an application for it for them. I do not know to whom the Knight of Kerry has given the reward; but this I can safely state, that none of the persons entitled to it received a shilling.

I have the honour to be, Sir,
Your obedient, humble servant,
Francis Twiss.

Note: A draft reply written on the back reads: 'Inform him that no reward was offered by Government, and that whatever was given at the recommendation of the Knight of Kerry was not to be considered as any claim on the part of the persons receiving it.'

FROM: *John FitzGerald, publican, Scartaglen, Co. Kerry.*
TO: *Under Sec., William Gregory, Dublin Castle.*

Scartaglen,
near Castleisland.
11th June, 1820

Sir,

I understand that several persons are applying for the reward offered by Government for the apprehension of Sullivan, the accomplice of Scanlan who murdered the woman on the Shannon last summer, and have been informed that the Knight of Kerry has absolutely got the money for some imposter who stated himself to be the person who arrested, or led to the arrest of, this man.

Now, Sir, I write this in order to let you know the whole truth; for I think when you know the story that you will say I have the best right to the money.

The fact is, Sir, I keep a public house in this village, and this Sullivan came to my house to drink, and gave me warrants which he said he got as part payment of his fortune, from his father-in-law, the bailiff of Lord Brandon, a man of the name of Houran, to whose daughter I know this man was married a short time before. I, accordingly, took the warrants for the whiskey, and Francis Twiss, Esq., of Castleisland, a magistrate of this county, having heard the story, had both Sullivan, alias Clifford, and me arrested; but I was bailed, and he, being a stranger, was sent to gaol, where he remained on this charge, and this only till some person from the banks of the Shannon came to gaol and knew him; so in this chance manner has this murderer been taken, and different persons now claim the reward.

The truth is, Sir, I am the person who was the cause of his arrest, and if any person deserves credit for his arrest, it is the magistrate, and if you take my advice, you will give me the reward, or give it to the magistrate to give it in charity, now that all our Banks are broken.

I am, honoured Sir,
Your most obedient servant,
John FitzGerald.

Note: Draft reply written on the back reads: 'No reward was ever offered by Government and no right can be claimed.'